The Runaway Princess

The RUNAWAY PRINCESS

Kate Coombs

FARRAR, STRAUS AND GIROUX
NEW YORK

Distributed in Canada by Douglas & McIntyre Ltd.
Printed in the United States of America
Designed by Jay Colvin
First edition, 2006
1   3   5   7   9   10   8   6   4   2

www.fsgkidsbooks.com

Library of Congress Cataloging-in-Publication Data
Coombs, Kate.
    The runaway princess / Kate Coombs.— 1st ed.
        p.   cm.
    Summary: Fifteen-year-old Princess Meg uses magic and her wits
to rescue a baby dragon and escape the unwanted attentions of princes
hoping to gain her hand in marriage through a contest arranged by
her father, the king.
    ISBN-13: 978-0-374-35546-3
    ISBN-10: 0-374-35546-0
    [1. Princesses—Fiction.   2. Contests—Fiction.   3. Dragons—
Fiction.   4. Magic—Fiction.   5. Fairy tales.]   I. Title.

PZ8.C788 Fif 2006
[Fic]—dc22

                                                    2005051225

For Carol Jean Cook Coombs,
my first and best reader

The Runaway Princess

PROLOGUE

WHEN MEG WAS SMALL, HER MOTHER USED TO tell her bedtime stories. Meg would sit up amid a pile of embroidered pillows, her five satin comforters already turned back by the castle maids. Queen Istilda would light the candles on top of the great carved dresser and come to sit beside her daughter's bed. With the sapphire bed curtains partly pulled, it was as if Meg had her own sky, light blue while the sky outside went dark. At such times the queen, who was not often seen without her needlework, would instead embroider the night with words.

"The princess stood at her window," the queen said on one particular evening, "longing for someone to come and save her, for the evil enchanter had bound her by his magic."

"Why didn't she break the spell?"

"She couldn't," Queen Istilda said gently. "Margaret, don't pick your nose."

Meg dropped her hand to the lap of her white satin nightgown. "Then what happened?"

"A handsome prince rode up to the castle gates."

"What did his horse look like?"

"White," Meg's mother said. "But a dreadful dragon had wound itself about the castle, and all those who tried to rescue the princess were slain."

Meg leaned forward, clasping her knees. "Couldn't someone sneak up on it from behind?"

The queen forged ahead. "The prince rode boldly toward the dragon, wielding the sword of the hero Lanolan."

"Where did he get it?" Meg asked. "Was Lanolan his father?"

"Stop interrupting, child," Meg's mother said in her most irritated voice, which still sounded like the cooing of doves, only four or five more doves than her ordinary voice.

Meg bit her lip and listened.

"Thank you," the queen said, folding her hands. "Now. The dragon raised its horrible head and cast fire at the young prince. But the brave prince used his shield and his sword to attack the loathsome beast."

"Maybe it was just hungry," Meg said.

"The dragon?" Queen Istilda asked, too shocked to remember that Meg was interrupting again. "They eat princesses!"

"It hadn't eaten this one, though," Meg pointed out.

"Darling, dragons are bad," the queen said.

Maybe, Meg thought, but she didn't say it. Instead she said, "If I were the princess, I would escape from the castle and defeat the wizard!"

"Margaret—"

"And if I were the prince—"

"The prince?" the queen asked, baffled.

"If I were the prince," Meg rushed on, "I'd sneak up behind the dragon and chop it in half before it could unwrap itself from around the castle!"

The queen opened her mouth and then closed it. "Well. I suppose we'll just end the story there."

Meg bounced a little on her bed, pleased.

The princess was six years old at the time. Soon after, her mother stopped telling her fairy tales. In time the queen forgot all about this odd conversation.

Perhaps she should have remembered.

I

MEG RAN ALONG A NARROW PATH TOWARD THE pond that lay hidden in the tall meadow grass northeast of the castle like a duckweed-colored button. Cam, the gardener's boy, came after her, having finished his weeding. Meg could hear frogs hitting the water and ducks scolding away into the rushes as they approached. When they reached the pond, they slowed and moved more quietly, crouching beside the water on opposite sides to catch tadpoles.

Cam scooped swiftly, then lifted his hands. "Got one!" he crowed, showing Meg the prisoner cupped in his palms.

Meg went him one better. She hitched up her skirts and started after the frogs themselves, like a pink satin heron. Her dress was a great hindrance.

Cam glanced over at her. "Don't you have anything less frilly?" he asked.

"I've told you before, it's all they give me." Meg lunged after another frog and missed.

"Maybe if you asked . . ." Cam suggested.

"And if I asked for armor and a sword?"

Cam slid his tadpole wriggling back into the pond. "I just wondered."

"They won't even let me go into Crown without a herd of soldiers and ladies. Anyway, there's something wrong with my parents."

"They're sick?"

"No, not that," Meg told him, knee-deep in water. "But my father spoke to me the other day."

"What did he say?"

"He inquired if I was well," Meg said portentously. Cam waited. "He said he wanted to talk to me sometime soon," she added.

Cam was still waiting. A dragonfly careened over the pond.

"That's all," Meg said with a shrug.

"Seems ordinary enough."

"No. It isn't. He hasn't noticed me in years." Which was why she never talked about him, not even with Cam. She had nothing to say.

Cam sat down in the grass and mud on the banks of the pond. "I'm sorry."

"I shouldn't complain. At least they're . . ." Meg pretended to see an intriguing new frog just to her right.

"Alive?" Cam said.

Meg blushed. Cam's parents were dead. His sister

had a small farm on the other side of the Witch's Wood. Did it matter terribly that Meg's father was busy being king of Greeve?

There really was a frog. Meg reached for it, but it sprang away and disappeared with an irate splash.

"I wish my mother *wouldn't* notice me," the princess said.

Cam waggled his brown feet in the water. "Why not? Sometimes you make no sense at all."

"Because," Meg snapped, "she's been making me embroider for days."

"Embroider?" Cam asked. "What for?"

Meg pretended to sew the air. "You know, stitchery? She calls it a 'wifely art.' " Meg imitated her mother's voice.

Cam snickered.

Dilly bustled along the hall, her arms full of towels. When she wasn't assisting Sterga, the fourth-floor housekeeper, with the linens, Dilly was Meg's maid. She was usually level-headed and cheerful, but she went all pink and worried as soon as Nort approached her.

"The princess is wanted in the throne room immediately, and *I'm* to help you find her!" Nort announced. It *would* be Nort, Dilly thought irritably. The younger housemaids called him Nort the Creep because he acted as though he was better than anyone, and eavesdropped and told tales to boot.

"Thank you, but I don't need any help." Dilly tried to leave him behind, but Nort followed.

"Guard Captain Hanak's orders," said Nort. Not that he was helping. He just trailed around after Dilly, poking his narrow nose into her business.

Dilly made a show of opening the door to one of the fourth-floor drawing rooms and closing it again.

"She's not there?" Nort asked in his oily, sarcastic voice.

Dilly spun around. "Go away!"

"They sent me to help," the apprentice guardsman repeated, leaning his scrawny frame against the nearest wall and folding his arms.

"You can help somewhere else!" Dilly hissed, folding her own arms.

Nort shrugged. "I would think the princess's personal maid would know where she is," he said. "I'll just go tell the king you can't find her."

"You can tell *Hanak* I'm still looking," Dilly answered. She didn't need to remind Nort that the guard captain was her uncle.

"When I'm a knight, you won't be allowed to talk to me like that," Nort told her.

"Knight? You'll be lucky to make senior guardsman," Dilly spat, but Nort was already slithering around the corner with a final pointy grin.

Dilly waited a moment or two before she hurried away in the opposite direction. She knew exactly where to find Meg. She just didn't want Nort knowing—or telling. On a day like this, when the sky was as blue as

Meg's best gown, the princess wouldn't be inside the castle. She would be out in the meadow with the gardener's
boy, ruining yet another dress.

Nort waited till he was out of sight of Meg's maid before
he ran all through the twisting corridors and slid to a
stop, breathless, beside the throne room doors.

"No sign of her?" Guard Captain Hanak asked
coldly.

Hanak was a compact, muscular man with a terrifying
blue stare. He'd made it clear he thought Nort got his
apprenticeship only because he was the prime minister's
third cousin once removed, a relationship the prime
minister himself seemed to have since forgotten. "No,
sir—Captain Hanak, sir," Nort said.

"Go back and look again," Hanak told him. Nort
scuttled away.

Hanak stuck his head into the throne room, where a
hundred colorfully dressed courtiers, merchants, and
hangers-on buzzed like a garden full of bees. The room
made a good garden, as it was hung from floor to ceiling with flower-filled tapestries. A closer look showed
knights dying tragically among the roses, but that was
proper chivalry for you.

At the end of the room, the king and his lady sat on
their great, uncomfortable thrones with as much grace as
possible—she looking like a hothouse plant in need of
water and he like a bad-tempered Percheron. The prime

minister caught sight of Hanak and pushed past a gaggle of ladies to reach him. Prime Minister Garald resembled an anemic accountant.

"Well?" Garald asked.

"Not yet," Hanak said quietly.

The prime minister bit his lip. "Where is she?"

"No one seems to know."

Garald made his way to the king's side.

"Have you found my daughter?" King Stromgard asked.

"I'm sorry, Your Majesty—" the prime minister began, but the king was turning to his wife.

"Istilda, you were supposed to get her dressed and curled for the occasion."

The queen grimaced. "You didn't say anything of the sort."

"It was implied."

"After twenty years, I still can't read your mind. Furthermore, as I told you this morning, I have a headache. I asked you to wait."

The king managed to look woeful and hopeful at the same time.

His wife relented. "Tell them to check the meadow," she said. "And you should play some music. Or feed these people."

"Just what would a royal princess be doing in a meadow?" King Stromgard asked.

"Embroidering a likeness of the flowers?" the prime minister put in.

"Enjoying the fresh spring air?" the queen suggested.

The king stood, and the room quieted. "The princess will join us shortly," he announced. "We will proceed to the dining hall to await her."

Meg dove after a frog and missed, falling flat on her face in the water. Cam laughed and laughed.

"It's not that funny," Meg told him, wringing out her heavy skirts.

"Yes it is." Then Cam's face changed, looking past her. "Uh-oh," he said.

"Uh-oh what?" Meg turned around. Dilly was halfway across the meadow, and even from here Meg could tell her maid was frantic. "Oh. Uh-oh," Meg agreed.

Ten minutes later, Cam was back in his garden, and Dilly was hurrying a soggy Meg up the steps to the castle. They came around a turn and stopped short at the sight of Nort rushing down.

"Ah. The missing princess," Nort said slyly.

"Nort?" Dilly asked.

"Yes, Dilly?" he said, smirking.

"Be very careful how you report the fact that the princess is dressing and will be along shortly." Her expression resembled Hanak's at that moment. As for Meg, even though she was still two steps below Nort, she looked down her nose at the apprentice guardsman.

Nort's smirk faded. "Yes, Dilly," he said, and made his escape.

"That Nort reminds me of a lizard," Meg remarked after he was gone. She ran into the castle and went dripping through half a dozen passageways, with Dilly trying not to slip on the damp floor behind her.

When they reached the princess's chambers, Dilly stifled a shriek. Dresses were strewn every which way, on and under the bed, across chairs, and in friendly heaps and sad little solo piles of skirt and sleeves like headless dolls. "What have you done now?"

"I was looking for something less lacy," Meg confessed.

"But I just tidied up this morning!" Dilly wailed, her black hair falling from its usual neat bun, her cheerful smile erased.

"I'm sorry, Dilly," Meg said sincerely.

Dilly took a deep breath and mustered a weak smile. "Well, we'd best find a dry dress, the least wrinkled one. Or rather, I'll find a dress while you wash the bog water out of your hair."

And so it was that a scant half hour later, Princess Margaret of Greeve walked into the dining hall dressed in a green satin gown that only Cam would have thought was frog-colored. With her hair combed up and her face washed, she looked nearly ladylike. A fresh murmur spread through the gathering as the princess made her way across the room. Faces turned toward her from each of the tables. Meg could feel herself flushing as she sank into an empty seat beside her mother.

King Stromgard leaned across the queen. "What have you been doing, Margaret?" he rumbled.

On the other side of the king, the prime minister whispered, "You *did* tell her, didn't you?"

The king sat back before Meg could answer, but the queen gave her daughter a quelling sideways look. "We were waiting for you, all of us, in the throne room."

"I'm sorry, Mother," she said, reaching for her soup spoon. Everyone else was finishing their roast peacock. Far too many curious eyes were upon Meg. Why hadn't anyone told her they were having a state dinner?

Meg's soup was cold. Behind her, a minstrel sang in a reedy voice about a prince who sailed across three seas to fetch his ladylove, only to find that she had turned into a pigeon and flown across the same seas the other way to find him.

Up the table, Garald peered at the king. "Did you, Your Majesty?"

The king lifted his bread with a mutter.

"You didn't," Garald breathed. "Not even a little warning?"

In spite of all the talk along the table, the queen heard. "Didn't what?" she asked her husband.

Beleaguered, the king tugged nervously at his beard. "More of a woman's role, eh, Istilda?"

"What is it this time?" she asked him. Her eyes widened. "No! You promised!"

"Not the proper—later, my dear," he replied.

"I'll admit I was surprised to see her so calm," the queen told the king.

"What's the matter?" Meg asked on the other side of her mother, but Istilda shook her head grimly. Uneasy, Meg returned to the task of catching up to the rest of the company without devouring her food like a wild boar.

She glanced down the table. An elderly knight was flirting quaintly with one of the queen's ladies-in-waiting, who pretended to be pleased. An earl's son was watching Meg. He smiled when he saw her looking. Meg concentrated on taking another bite of scallop salad.

Soon enough Meg finished her dinner, just in time for her father to make one of his long speeches. Meg wondered if Cam would be able to escape from Chief Gardener Tob in the morning. Then again, her mother seemed to be feeling better, so tomorrow would probably be full of uneven stitches and snagged threads. Meg sighed.

"I remind you that your interests are my interests," the king proclaimed, sounding like the prime minister. "As a kingdom, we must unite our efforts to accomplish the greatest growth and progress in our illustrious history."

Garald probably wrote the speech, Meg decided. He looked very proud. Was he mouthing the words under his breath?

"We can put an end to this slight yet worrisome economic slowdown even as we rid ourselves of the baleful scourges upon our fair land," the king continued, "freeing up valuable real estate with a great deal of potential."

What scourges? Meg wondered. Some of the courtiers whispered to one another, probably asking the same thing.

"In addition, the events embodying the solution to these blights will generate much-needed income as an influx of spectators with their pockets full of gold flock eagerly to spend their money in the noble city of Crown."

Spectators? "What is Father talking about?" Meg asked.

"Shh," said Queen Istilda.

Garald was definitely mouthing the words.

The king raised his hands dramatically. "A dragon darkens our dells. A witch haunts our woods. Bandits roam our moors."

"It's not that bad," Meg whispered.

"*Shh,*" Queen Istilda said with a severe expression that seemed out of place on her porcelain face.

Meg slumped in her chair.

"But with the help of our fair daughter"—Meg straightened—"we can transform our beleaguered kingdom into a new and shining realm."

Meg looked at her mother, utterly baffled. The queen avoided her eyes.

King Stromgard swept on. "In the great tradition of so many monarchs, I offer my daughter's hand in marriage and half my kingdom to the prince who can rid us of these evils, restoring peace and prosperity to our realm."

The crowd burst into applause, covering Meg's horrified response. "I won't!" She jumped to her feet. Everyone smiled up at her, still clapping. The king stood, too, and put his arm around her. The entire court cheered, calling Meg's name, as the king led his bristling daughter out of the room.

2

HE ROYAL FAMILY OF GREEVE DISCUSSED THE matter in the king's study—if you could call a loud quarrel a discussion. The family portraits looked pained.

"It's for the good of the kingdom," her father said for the seventh time.

"It's crazy and old-fashioned and I won't do it!" Meg yelled.

The king turned to his wife. "You tell her."

"Margaret," Queen Istilda said softly. "You're fifteen now, of an age to be married." She stepped to her daughter's side.

"You weren't married till you were twenty!" Meg blazed, moving away.

"I was an old maid," the queen said, stricken.

"It's for the good of the kingdom," her father said again.

"I'm sure your clever prime minister can think of a better plan," Meg told him nastily.

Garald and the king shook their heads.

"I'm sorry," Garald said, "but it's for—"

"—the good of the kingdom?" Meg inquired.

"I was going to say timber and tract housing," Garald explained. "Replenishing Greeve's sadly depleted treasury."

"Is that all?" Meg inquired sarcastically.

The king's brows lowered. "Enough of this mollycoddling!" he roared. "You are a princess, and you will act like one!"

"I quit!" Meg told him. "Find yourself another princess!"

"You can't quit our family," the queen said, her eyes filling up with tears.

"Oh yes I can," Meg muttered, heading for the door.

Her father blocked her. "Margaret, I offer you one last chance to play willingly the part that life has assigned you."

Meg glared up at him. "No," she said.

The queen wiped her eyes.

"There's more," King Stromgard told his daughter, folding his arms. "Tradition suggests that the princess be sequestered in a tower until her hand is won."

Meg gaped.

Queen Istilda turned pale. "Our own daughter? A prisoner?"

The king drew himself up. "It would not be necessary had our own daughter seen fit to fulfill her royal duty."

"But the only tower we have—" the queen began.

The king stalked to the window. Across the east meadow, a single stone tower jutted against the dark green of the forest. "It will do."

"It's filthy!" Queen Istilda objected, weeping still more.

Shaken, Meg stepped to her father's side. "You're going to lock me up?"

"It's sequestering," he insisted gruffly, patting her arm. "I suggest you have the tower cleaned," he told his wife. To Garald he said, "Have Hanak guard her till it's ready, or she might just run off." King Stromgard swept out of the room.

"I told him he'd have to take measures," the prime minister said with a smarmy smile.

"Do be quiet!" the queen snapped.

That night Meg slept in a little bedroom without any windows and with only one door. Hanak, who was usually rather grim, seemed sorry for her, but he did his duty, as always. She wasn't even allowed to see Dilly.

"But Dilly's my maid!" Meg protested.

"She has other responsibilities at present," the captain of the guard said uncomfortably. He looked around and lowered his voice. "Truth be told, she's cleaning that tower for you."

It was a long night. "At least the tower will have a window," Meg said to the stones.

As it turned out, she spent a whole week in that room. Her mother brought her some embroidery, but she threw it against the wall and wouldn't talk.

"My dear, your father means you no harm," Queen Istilda said, sounding doubtful. Meg closed her eyes to block out her mother's anxious gaze and flopped onto the bed.

The queen sat down beside her daughter. "We would have seen you married in a year or two even without this—this contest."

Meg lay still.

"And isn't it a tiny bit romantic to have handsome young men travel from far and wide to vie for your hand?" her mother asked. Meg refused to answer.

The queen stood. "Margaret, you're just going to have to get used to the idea," she said. She left with a disappointed sigh.

Later, Meg found the embroidery and stitched at it simply because she was so bored. After that she pretended to sword-fight—her opponent the prime minister died very bloodily.

Then it was time for the prisoner's next meal. At least it was Meg's favorite, chicken pie with carrots and blackberries. Cam had no doubt grown the carrots, Meg thought, biting into her dinner.

Ten minutes later, Meg was snoring heartily, her nose in the last bit of pie. The door opened.

"Are you sure she's all right?" the queen asked, rushing to wipe the pie from her daughter's face.

"Quite sure," Hanak said.

When Meg woke up, sunlight streamed in through a window. She ran to look out, to look down. She was in the tower. They must have put sleep drops in her dinner. "So I wouldn't make a scene," she remarked coldly, going back to the bed and reaching under it for the chamber pot.

Next she went to the window again and leaned over the ledge. Below her she could see the pale top of someone's head. Hanak had black hair like Dilly's. "Hello," she called.

Whoever it was stepped away from the tower wall. "Nort?" Meg said, shocked. "What are you doing down there?"

Nort held up an oversized spear. "Guarding you. What does it look like?"

"You are *not* my guard!" Meg cried.

"Am too."

"Are not."

"Am too."

Meg paused. "Where's Hanak?"

"He's busy at the castle," Nort said. "You've got me. Royal orders."

"I'll give you a royal order, Nort the Short," Meg announced. "Go shoot yourself in the knees with a crossbow!"

Nort laughed. "Come down and make me."

With a furious strangled noise, Meg withdrew into the tower. She took a deep breath and surveyed her new domain.

Dilly had done a good job. When Meg and Cam had explored the tower last summer, it had been bare of everything but cobwebs and bats. They were planning to use it as a spies' den, but Hanak found out somehow and locked the place up. Now the curving stone walls were clean and hung with tapestries Meg thought she recognized from one of the guest rooms in the castle. Bed, chair, a little divan, a table. On the table, a noxious pile of embroidery—it followed her everywhere! A pitcher and a glass. A plate with a knife and spoon. A candle in a brass holder. Two extra candles. A flint and steel. Ah, and books. Meg hurried to pick them up. *Proper Etiquette for Princesses*, *500 Years of Royal Weddings*, *Fine Stitchery for the Noble Fair* . . . Meg shuddered, dropping the books.

She went to the door, already knowing how sturdy and locked it would be. Beyond it, she knew, a steep stairway wound down to another door below. It, too, would be locked.

Meg returned to the window and gazed out over the meadow at the castle, imagining her father and mother at their noontime meal, surrounded by conversation, able to come and go as they pleased. Soon another picture crept into her mind, one of dozens of princes riding their horses along dozens of roads, over high mountains and through low valleys, past the city and up to the castle gates.

Meg sighed gloomily. It wasn't that she minded princes, as long as they stayed out of her way. No, what she felt was envy—she wanted to be riding a horse herself. She would travel across the mountains and into the next kingdom, and the kingdom after that, her faithful squire Cam by her side . . . He could ride a mule or something.

Meg went over to the bed to stifle her tears so Nort wouldn't hear her. Then she lay dry-eyed, considering. There had to be a way to get out of this place.

After a while Meg woke to a noise. When she remembered where she was, she hurried to the window. Meg smiled for the first time all day. Cam was below the tower, arguing with Nort. As anyone would be.

"Cam!" she called, waving madly.

Cam waved back at her. Nort made a grab for the basket Cam was holding, but Cam swung it away.

Nort shook his spear in what was meant to be a threatening manner. "I'm the guard, and I give her anything she's to get."

"No," Cam said firmly, "you're the guard and you guard. They sent me with her food, and I'm supposed to deliver it. I was told how and everything."

"Says who?" Nort tried to loom over Cam, but Cam was half a head taller.

"Says Hanak," Cam explained. "Who do you think pulled me away from my weeding? He told me you're too busy with your new duties, or you'd be running errands still."

Nort couldn't help looking pleased at that. Cam took advantage of the moment. "There's a little pulley up top," he said. "She's to lower it, and I'll pop her food in and send it back up. Ready, Princess Margaret?" he asked her solemnly.

Meg smiled again at Cam's use of her formal name. She found the mechanism beside the window and began to wind it down—a metal basket like a birdcage on a fine chain descended, clattering. She stopped it partway. "Can't you just bring my meals up the stairs?"

Cam shook his head. "Hanak's orders. Besides, he says your father has the only key."

It was not good news, but it was useful information.

"Enough chatter," Nort said, trying to take charge.

Meg wound the cage the rest of the way down. Cam placed the wicker basket inside, and she pulled the contraption up again.

"Be off, now," Nort proclaimed instantly.

Cam ignored this. "Are you all right, Princess?"

"Not really," Meg said. "Thanks for asking."

"Tomorrow you're to send down the chamber pot, as well," Cam added.

"Ugh."

Then Nort really did chase Cam off. Or at least, Cam let him think so. Meg's friend waved goodbye and loped cheerfully across the meadow. Finally he was gone. Meg felt a pang of loneliness without him.

"That boy is far too familiar with you, Princess," Nort observed.

"*You* are far too familiar," she told him, pulling the basket inside the tower.

Meg sat down to eat. She lifted the cloth, noting its exquisite embroidery with disdain. She took out the food. It must be meant to last the rest of the day: half a baked chicken, a loaf of bread, three boiled eggs, a dish filled with squash and peas, a little pot of plum preserves . . . She saw a small note tucked under the eggs. Meg opened it quickly, forgetting her hunger.

It was written on a scrap of parchment in Cam's scrawl. *I'll com bak.* Nothing more. But Meg beamed. She *would* get out of the tower. She just needed a little help.

Newly hopeful, Meg passed the afternoon as best she could. She ate some bread and watched the birds. She ignored both Nort and the embroidery. She managed to read a bit of the book about royal weddings. When she found an account of a princess who ran away the night before her marriage, Meg thought it was a very good sign.

Much later, Meg heard a strange sound outside. She went to the window. Cam was grinning up at her. Nort lay on the grass, his spear placed neatly beside him.

"What did you do to him?" Meg asked, alarmed and pleased.

"He tripped," Cam said.

"But if he tells—" Meg began.

"He didn't see me. I came around through the woods and snuck up behind him while he was practicing being a daring knight with that spear of his."

"Good. Now get me down."

"How?"

"With a rope, silly!"

Cam nodded. "And then what?"

"Then I can run away!"

Cam looked worried. "If you don't pull the food up, they'll come to the top to see what's wrong."

"So?" Meg said scornfully.

"Everyone will go out searching for you."

"I can't stay here!"

"No, I suppose not." He didn't sound convinced.

"Kings and princes," Meg muttered. "The way they're going on, we won't have any Dragon Crags, Witch's Wood, or Dreadful Moor."

"Just Crags, Wood, and Moor?" Cam asked, trying to keep a straight face.

"Cam! I won't marry some bread-for-brains who goes around killing innocent dragons!"

"Innocent dragons?" It wasn't a common expression.

"The poor creature hasn't come down the mountain in two years," she argued. "And then it only stole an ox. It hasn't eaten a princess since my great-aunt was a girl. And the witch!" Meg was waving her hands now, talking faster. "Love potions, wart hexes, nothing awful."

"What about those frogs?" Cam asked.

"That's just gossip," Meg told him. "It isn't fair!"

"The bandits are trouble," Cam put in halfheartedly. Meg's mouth dropped open. "They steal from the rich and give to the poor! Just last month I was Bold Rodolfo and you were his Merry Band!"

Cam lifted his hands. "All right, all right. What does any of that have to do with you?"

"Don't you see?" Meg asked, suddenly inspired. "We must save them."

"Save who?"

"The dragon. The witch. The bandits. We must save them from the evil princes."

"Evil princes?" Cam laughed. "Maybe you'd like those princes, once you got to know them." He struck a heroic pose. "I am Prince Stoutneck, come to capture your heart, fair maiden of lo, such royal blood!"

"You're mocking me."

Nort stirred in the grass. They both looked at him, but he merely sighed and lay still.

"Come *on*," she said, leaning dangerously far out of the window in her eagerness to persuade Cam. "We can rescue the baleful scourges together! And I'll tell my father, 'Ha *ha*! *I* have won the contest! You shall send this pack of foolish princes on their way!' "

Cam laughed again. "I'll get you down," he said. "I promise. But we have do it so that they think you're still up there." He poked Nort idly with one foot. "Give me time to come up with something."

"Cam!" Meg wailed.

"I'll write you a note every day."

Meg waved wanly as Cam turned to go. "Wait," she

called. Cam looked back up at her. "Dilly will help us," she told him.

"Are you sure?"

"I'm sure."

"I'll ask her," Cam promised. "Don't worry. It won't be long."

Meg felt her throat closing, but she didn't let herself cry. Cam was being horribly sensible. All she really needed was a piece of rope.

3

HE SUN WAS SHINING ON THE GRASS. BIRDS were calling across the meadow. Nort sat up, groggy.

"I'm going to tell my father you were sleeping on the job," a voice said above him.

Nort jumped to his feet. "Someone attacked me!"

"He's not going to believe that," Meg told him. "I don't believe it, and I've been up here the whole time."

Nort touched his aching head. "My head . . ."

"It's still there."

"I was struck! Struck down from behind!"

"Right," Meg jeered. "The terrible monster struck you, took your spear away, and kidnapped the princess."

Nort looked down at his spear, then up at the princess.

"Maybe you had a bad dream," Meg suggested in kinder tones. "Maybe you bumped your head on the wall when you fell asleep."

Nort stared up at her. "Maybe," he said. "You won't—will you really tell?"

"No. You must be very bored. If I were you, I'd have dozed off, too." She disappeared into the tower room.

Nort jumped at shadows all afternoon, till he was finally relieved by a dour older guard as darkness fell.

Days passed, and the castle began to fill up with princes. Dilly ran about the castle with her stack of linens, making up beds for the guests. Not only princes, but endless retinues of men-at-arms and servants wandered up and down the halls. The castle was nearly bursting when some of the southern princes set up camp west of it, tethering their steeds beside their tents. The encampment grew, even drawing some of the princes out of the castle to join their rivals in the fresh air.

Meg hung out the tower window one afternoon, trying to imagine the tents Nort had told her were spread on the other side of the castle. She hated waiting. Dilly's and Cam's notes said they were working on a plan, but nothing had happened yet. So here she sat, like a dungeon prisoner, except for being higher up and probably cleaner. Her only consolation was that Dilly had sent her a skipping rope. When she grew sick of reading the book on royal weddings and watching the birds, Meg took off her bulky gown and skipped rope in her monogrammed bloomers. The *thwack* of the rope against the floor confused Nort no end.

Her mother had come to see her once, the second

day of her imprisonment, but Meg refused to come to the window, and the queen hadn't returned.

Meg sighed, remembering. Then a figure on horseback caught her attention. A young man came galloping across the meadow, reining up just short of squashing Nort. Meg frowned and stepped out of sight. She had often thought of squashing Nort herself, but a stranger had no right to do it. She peered out.

"Hold," Nort squeaked, raising his spear protectively.

"You guard the princess?" the young man inquired.

"I do," said Nort. "You're not to come around here till the end of the contest."

"What, no wooing the maiden?" The stranger was dark-haired, slender, and very handsome. Meg's heart bumped, but she quickly reminded herself what he was doing here.

"No wooing," Nort said, blushing.

"So tell me, what's she like?" the visitor asked Nort.

"I'm right up here listening!" Meg called, insulted into partly abandoning her royal dignity. She kept her face in the shadow of the window frame, though. She wouldn't be gawked at.

The stranger tipped his head back, smiling up at the window. "Beg pardon, Princess," he said pleasantly. "I am Prince Bain, and I offer you my greetings."

"Oh. Hello," Meg said. She recovered a bit. "But you're really not allowed."

"Very well," the prince said. "Good day, my lady!"

Before she could answer, he wheeled his horse and started away. He looked positively dashing racing across the meadow.

"Hmmph!" said Meg. "He's after the kingdom," she told herself.

"I sent him off, that one," Nort said righteously.

"Of course you did." Meg nearly picked up the embroidery, she was that flustered.

Word must have gotten around. Five more princes came to the tower that morning, with Nort trying in vain to keep them away. Meg soon avoided the window altogether, making her even more irritable. As no one actually caught a glimpse of her, more and more princes showed up in hopes of seeing the mysterious Margaret.

Finally Hanak got wind of it and told the prime minister, who sent a messenger around to all of the royal visitors telling them that anyone who didn't stay away from the princess's tower till the end of the contest would be immediately disqualified. Things quieted down after that.

Dear Dilly, Meg wrote the next day. *Some princes were creeping about the tower yesterday. All of them were rude and ugly.* Meg crossed her fingers, remembering the dark-haired prince. *Are you ever going to get married?*

Dear Meg, Dilly wrote back. *Not all of the princes are ugly, but they want too many towels. I might get married someday. Right now I'm busy with towels. P.S. Be patient. Cam and I are making a plan.*

Tomorrow, Meg thought grimly, I'm going to rip up these dresses and make my own rope. She lost herself in visions of dropping the book of etiquette on Nort's head and climbing down the tower wall, clever as a spider. Visions of running away to a far-off kingdom all by herself.

Dilly and Cam sat glumly in a little gazebo in the center of the royal rose arbor. If anyone had found them, he might have thought the two were stealing kisses. Instead they were trying to decide how to steal a princess.

"We have to get her down," Cam said. "She hates it up there, and we *promised*."

"They'll know," Dilly informed him.

Cam tucked back a trailing branch of roses with a practiced hand. "We need some kind of a trick. But I can't think of one."

"If you were her guard instead of Nort . . ." Dilly began.

"If we had a flying carpet . . ." said Cam.

"If we had an extra princess . . ." said Dilly.

"If we had the key . . ." said Cam.

A breeze drifted the scent of roses through the gazebo. "After she pulls up her food, we've got a whole day," Dilly mused.

"For what?"

"To get her down and back up again."

"Let's just start with the getting-down part," Cam said. "Three heads are better than two."

"That's true . . ." Dilly said slowly.

"Do you have an idea?" Cam asked.

Early the next morning, Cam came across the meadow with the basket of food. Nort looked sleepy, having just come on duty. He had taken to dropping his spear in the grass and slouching against the tower with his arms folded.

"Good morning, Princess!" Cam called.

Meg was sitting cross-legged on the floor ripping up a mustard-colored gown, but she came to the window when she heard Cam's voice. "Good morning!"

"You might say good morning to me," Nort told her testily.

"Never mind that," Cam said to the apprentice guardsman. "I need your help."

"What?" Nort asked, surprised. "Why would I help you?"

Meg's expression mirrored Nort's. All that waiting, and *this* was their plan? Then the princess saw Dilly.

"Because you're bored," Cam informed him. "Also because you might disappear into the woods and never be found if you don't."

Nort reached uneasily for his spear, but it was gone. "What are you talking about?"

Meg smiled. One way or another, it was going to work.

"We're here to help the princess," Cam said. "You do like the princess, don't you?"

Nort looked up, catching Meg's eye. "Well . . ."

"Good," said Cam. "We're going to get her out of the tower, and you're going to join us."

"Who's we?" Nort made a sideways move, but Cam was faster, standing very close. "You can't do this!" Nort cried.

"We can if you help us," a voice behind Nort said evenly as a spearpoint touched his back.

Nort spun around instinctively. The spear scraped his arm and ended up just over his heart. "Dilly?" he asked, bewildered by the sight of a small, angry lady's maid. "No! You can't make me! I'm true to my duty! To the death!" he said wildly.

"Lower the spear, please," came Meg's voice from above. "Nort, don't you want to have an adventure?"

Dilly lowered the spear. Nort scowled.

"You do," said Cam. "Admit it."

"Or what? I could have you both thrown in the dungeon!" he said, sulky.

Dilly laughed. "I was changing the linens."

"I brought the princess her food and went back to work in the garden," Cam said, his face beaming with innocence.

"You bumped your head a bit too hard the other day. You're raving," Meg said sweetly.

"I still think we should dump him in the woods, at least till we're finished," Dilly remarked. "I brought extra rope." She pulled a coil of rope from a bag over her shoulder and dropped it on the ground. Cam produced an even heavier length of rope and threw it down, too.

"You're all crazy!" Nort hissed. He paused, curious. "What do you mean, adventure? Finished with what?"

It took another fifteen minutes to convince Nort that theirs was the path of glory for anyone who really wanted to become a knight someday. Still, Meg noticed that Dilly didn't offer to return the spear. And Cam insisted Nort swear an oath of allegiance to Meg and her purposes.

"Purposes?" Nort asked anxiously.

Dilly hefted the spear. "You know what happens to knights who fail to keep their oaths, don't you?"

"Of course," Nort declared. Meg suspected he didn't, but at least Nort seemed suitably impressed.

After a bit more discussion, Meg lowered the wire basket so Cam could tie his rope to it. Then she pulled the basket up and removed the rope, retying it carefully to the bedpost. She thought it would probably hold her weight.

For the ninth or tenth time, the others made sure no one was coming. "It's all right," Dilly said. Meg began to clonk and scramble her way down the tower wall.

"You're going to . . . !" called Cam.

Meg bounced against a sharp stone. "Oof! Tell me a bit—ow—sooner!"

"We can't leave the rope here. Arbel will see," Nort said.

"The night guard?" Dilly asked.

"The night guard."

"We need it in case she has to go back up," said Dilly.

"Just a little farther!" Cam told the princess.

Meg caught her skirt on a rusty hook and tipped sideways. The fabric ripped as she managed to right herself. With a final slide, a rope burn, and a thump, Meg traveled the last ten feet to the bottom of the tower. "Free!" she announced, lifting her arms exultantly and twirling about.

"Now help us think," said Dilly. "What about the rope?"

"It's nearly the same color as the stones," Meg said.

"So they won't be able to see it from the castle."

"Maybe not," said Cam. "But they'll expect to see candlelight up here in the evening."

"She'll just have to come back every night before the changing of the guard," Dilly said. "She can pull the rope up and then bring it out the next morning when Nort's here again."

They all looked at Meg. "I'm not going back!" she proclaimed.

"You have to sleep *somewhere*," Dilly said.

"But I just got out!"

"The point is, it will buy you days and days of freedom," Cam told the princess.

"It will be much easier for all concerned," Nort added, determined to join the conversation.

They were ganging up on her now. "But—"

"It wouldn't have to be you, even," Cam added, glancing over at Dilly.

Dilly folded her arms. "Oh no no no. I'm not going up that thing."

"In an emergency," Cam said, "you could."

"Right," Meg told her, "in an emergency."

Dilly glowered. "Let's not have any of those, then." She changed the subject, handing her bag to the princess. "You'd better change."

Meg flapped her shining skirt. "You think this might give me away?" She took the bag and disappeared around the tower into the edge of the Witch's Wood.

"What if somebody comes while she's not up there?" Nort asked.

"Just tell them she's in a snit and won't talk to anyone," Dilly told him.

Nort nodded fervently. "They'll believe that."

The others were leaning against the tower, all but dozing in the sunshine, when the princess came back. She looked like a castle servant now, unremarkable with her light brown hair, freckled nose, and greenish brown eyes. The dress was blue cotton and not quite ankle-length. The shoes were of sturdy leather. Meg handed the bag with her gown stuffed in it to Dilly.

"Better?" Cam asked, remembering Meg's feelings about satin skirts.

Meg grinned. "Better." She kicked out a foot. "The shoes are heavy."

"They'll take you farther than those thin slippers," Dilly said. "Let me fix your hair." Dilly braided Meg's hair tidily, completing the transformation.

"What are the princes up to?" Meg asked.

"Strutting around showing off their weapons," Cam said, disgusted.

"Bearing their arms like true heroes," Nort corrected. Cam ignored him.

"I want to see them," said Meg.

"You can't go inside!" Dilly exclaimed.

"Not the castle. I'll just walk between the tents."

"The princes don't know what she looks like," Cam pointed out.

Dilly gave her approval only after Meg had agreed to wear Dilly's scarf and carry the food basket. "You'll be hungry later, and it adds nicely to your disguise." Dilly wanted to come along, but she had to get her work done. Cam said he'd accompany Meg.

"What about me?" Nort asked plaintively.

"You've got to stay here with the invisible princess," Cam told him.

Nort turned woeful. "It's not much of an adventure."

"Ah, but soon I'll be sending you and Cam out on night forays," Meg said, lowering her voice.

Cam winced, but Nort brightened. "That's all right, then. What's the plan, anyway? You said you had a plan."

Meg surveyed her co-conspirators. "We're going to keep those princes from winning the contest."

4

EG AND CAM WANDERED THROUGH THE EN-
campment, joining a crowd of gawkers from the
city and courtiers from the castle, as well as
vendors hawking berry pastries, souvenir dragon fig-
urines, and good-luck charms conveniently composed of
sticks and pebbles. To Meg's relief, no one gave her a
second glance.

Most of the princes had come out into the sunshine
to practice sparring, flashing their swords for the benefit
of an admiring populace. One prince had even set up a
wooden dragon and was methodically shooting arrows at
it. "I don't think a real dragon would stand still to be
made into a porcupine," Meg told Cam behind her
hand.

She heard a twittering of merchant girls ahead. Beyond them, a tall, handsome prince with wavy blond hair
and an arrogant mouth was looking off into the distance.

"It's him," one of the girls said. "Prince Vantor of Rogast!"

Another girl giggled. "Have you got it?"

A third girl pulled an embroidered cloth out of her market basket. The other two helped her raise the little banner. Meg and Cam walked past to read the lettering. *Prince Vantor the Valiant!!!!!* it said in curling letters adorned with forget-me-nots.

"Prince Vantor!" one of the girls squealed hopefully. The prince turned his head, lifting a single aristocratic brow. With a curt nod, he went into the nearest tent, a dark gray one with blue and gold trim. The girls ran off in a chorus of tee-hee-hees.

Meg rolled her eyes as she slowed with Cam beside the tent to listen.

"Another gaggle of geese, my lord?" said a rasping voice.

"Let's hope this princess is more pleasing in manner, Horace," a deep voice responded.

"They say she is seventeen and very beautiful," the first man said.

"They also say she is forty and resembles a turnip," the prince told his manservant. "Which would be unfortunate, but nevertheless beside the point."

Meg's face was a study.

"If I may ask, Your Highness, what is the point?"

"Winning," the prince replied.

Meg and Cam moved on.

A weak-chinned prince was fencing with a large, hairy one while a pleasant-looking royal with rumpled brown hair called out suggestions. A fat prince wrapped in furs despite the heat addressed his servants angrily in an odd clicking tongue. A lanky, bearded prince flipped a knife over and over, watching the others. There were even twin princes, two big smiling brothers who laughed and slapped each other on the back. Meg and Cam walked along behind them.

"Do you think she's pretty?" asked one twin.

"They're always pretty," the other said.

"But what if she's not? What if she's the only ugly one ever? Maybe she's under a curse, and that's why they hid her in the tower."

Meg opened her mouth to speak, but Cam jabbed her and she caught herself.

"Dorn, they're always pretty," said the second twin.

Prince Dorn spotted Meg and Cam. "You there!"

"Yes, sir?" Cam asked. Meg stared down at the ground, trying to disguise her irritation along with her royal visage.

"Are you from town?"

"We work in the castle gardens," Cam said quickly.

Dorn nudged his twin. "They've come out to see the spectacle, eh, Dagle?"

"Is this your girl?" Dagle asked.

"She's my sister," Cam blurted. "She's shy."

Prince Dagle beamed at the top of Meg's head, then

turned his attention back to Cam. "So, lad, what do you think of the contest?"

"He can tell at a glance who's going to win!" Dorn said.

Cam took the hint. "You seem likely candidates."

"Right you are!" Dorn crowed.

"But, sir," Cam ventured, "there are two of you."

"Right again!" said Dagle.

"If you win . . ." Cam's voice trailed off.

The twins looked baffled.

"There's only one princess," Cam told them pointedly. Meg's face turned red.

"Oh. Ha-ha!" The princes guffawed, putting their arms across each other's shoulders. "You want to know a secret?" Dagle asked, leaning closer to Cam.

"Sure."

"When we win, we'll flip a coin!" he explained.

Meg grabbed Cam's arm so hard he winced.

"Very clever," Cam managed to say. "If you'll excuse us . . ." He pulled Meg away. The twin princes were still laughing as they left. Cam pried Meg's hand loose from his arm.

"*Cam!*" was all she could say, outraged.

"You wanted to see them," he reminded her.

"Yes, I did," Meg said through gritted teeth.

Meg and Cam walked past a black tent embroidered with silver rams, then a bright blue tent hung about with birdcages. The birds were calling in what sounded like human speech, but neither Meg nor Cam knew what language. Meg forgot her anger in trying to decipher the words.

They slowed again to watch an earnest scribe interviewing a stocky little redheaded prince. "So I said, 'Hey, I can do this. Just give me your fastest horse,' " the prince said dramatically.

"And what did he say?" the scribe inquired, managing to write as he talked.

The prince strutted about like a red-combed rooster. "He said, 'My son, you are needed here.' "

"And you . . ."

"And I said, 'Father, I'll come home real soon with half a kingdom and a gorgeous girl.' "

Meg gave Cam a sideways look.

"And he . . ."

"And he said, 'Very well,' " the prince concluded.

"That's marvelous," the scribe bubbled. "Could I get a final quote?"

The prince lifted his head still higher. "Tell the populace: I, Prince George the Fourth of Shervelhame, will bring glory to this kingdom, to my father's realm, and to myself."

Meg and Cam smothered their snickers as they moved on. They wound between a dour, graying prince, one with an oversize powdered wig, and a cluster of ale-drinking men in orange livery. Gradually they made their way out of the encampment.

Then Cam's attention was caught by two men under a tree. Like the others, they were well dressed and well groomed. But they also seemed—Cam tried to decide what. Watchful, perhaps, unlike the rest of this lot. "Notice anything different about those two?"

"That's Prince Bain." Meg's voice sounded peculiar, and Cam glanced over at her, surprised.

"Let's find out what they're saying," he told her. Meg and Cam circled around and came up behind the men, edging closer and closer, wriggling through the long grass until they were at the base of the tree behind their quarry. They hunkered down to listen.

"No trouble?" one man said.

"None," said the other.

"You look well, Prince Bain."

"Thank you," the prince answered, as if he were amused. "Now go see what you can find out."

"And you?" the first man asked.

"I'll make my own inquiries."

Meg and Cam lay flat, waiting for the men to leave. When they had, Cam sat up to stare at Meg. "You *know* that prince?"

Meg flushed. "He came around the tower the other day. On a horse."

"That's all?"

"It was a nice horse," Meg said defensively.

"Hmmph." Cam stood up. "I've got to get back. My cabbages are a bit peaky."

"You sound like a worried mother," Meg told him.

"But they're yellowish around the edges," Cam explained.

Meg rose and brushed off her skirt. "I'll come with you."

Cam shook his head. "Tob will recognize you."

"I'll walk partway," she offered.

They strode along in silence. Finally Cam said, "So, now you've seen them. What do you think?"

They came across a stableboy, and Meg ducked her head. When they were well past him, Cam asked her again. "So?"

"They're big and old and gruff and vain."

"That Prince Bain isn't so bad," Cam said casually.

"He's at least eighteen! Maybe even nineteen!"

"True," Cam replied. They stopped, having reached the rose arbor. "What are you going to do now?"

"I'll go and find the witch," Meg told him. "Or the dragon. I've got to warn them."

"Meg, there's no warning dragons. You know they *eat* princesses, don't you?"

She tossed her head. "Legend has it."

"Your great-aunt? She was only a year older than you when the creature gobbled her up."

"Perhaps it wasn't the dragon. It might have been a nefarious plot implicating the dragon."

"Or," Cam insisted, "it was the dragon."

Meg set her jaw.

"At least wait till tomorrow to look for it," he said. "I'll come with you."

"What about Tob?" she snapped.

"He's off to his brother-in-law's funeral tonight."

Meg relented. "All right. Today I'll warn the witch."

Cam began to go through the gate, but Meg was still standing there. "What is it?" he asked.

"They talked about me like—like I don't know what," Meg said awkwardly.

"Like you're not you," Cam told her, and Meg nodded.

Cam examined her. "You don't look anything like a turnip."

Meg had to smile.

The woods were full of sunlight and birdsong. As well as brambles, Meg discovered when she tore her skirt coming up behind the witch's cottage. Its walls were ancient and weather-beaten, its thatch sagged picturesquely, and a little hand-lettered sign read GO AWAY. Curtains hung at the windows, black ones adorned by neat rows of white skulls.

Meg crouched against the back wall, slowly raising her head until she could see in the window. The inside of the cottage was dim. She could make out the shape of a fireplace cradling what must be the witch's cauldron. She wondered what simmered in the pot. There was a sofa. An armchair. And dozens of little blobby shapes . . . Meg heard a croaking sound. One of the blobs leaped across the room.

Many an old woman lived in a small house cluttered with memories and twining fondly with cats. Gorba the Witch had filled her home with clutter, true enough—

dainty dishes patterned with sprigs of noxious herbs, china statuettes of monstrous pagan deities, samplers cross-stitched with sayings like *Have an apple, dearie!* But she owned not a single cat. Instead, Gorba's cottage was full of frogs.

A great bullfrog sat on a cushion near the hearth like a venerable monarch. A bevy of leopard frogs and spring peepers dripped on the sofa. Gorba had wood frogs and painted frogs, puddle frogs and reed frogs, rockets and golden-backs and squeakers, even a rare tomato frog. Tiny tree frogs clung to the curtains like jewels. An ornate bathtub full of pond water stood in one corner, and several frogs were practicing diving into a round tin laundry tub nearby. Frog songs called across the room. Flies buzzed all unsuspecting through the open window.

Meg had never seen so many frogs in one place. She watched the frogs, waiting for a sign of the witch herself. "Must be out," Meg said to herself.

After which a creaking voice behind her inquired, "Well? Have you come to buy or to spy?"

Meg spun around. The witch was older than old, with flashing black eyes and a bulgy nose like a small potato. Her hair was a peculiar shade of violet shot with shadows.

"Neither," Meg said, taking a step back.

"Selling something, are you?" The witch's eyes narrowed.

"Oh no, not that. It's about the king's contest." Meg waited a moment. "Haven't you heard?"

"I don't want to enter," the witch said. "I prefer the quiet life. What's it for, an ocean voyage? A year's supply of barley?"

Meg wasn't sure how to answer. She didn't want to tell the entire story. *Well, Madam Witch, I'm the prize.* "Half the kingdom and all that," she explained. "They've called a bunch of princes over to complete three tasks."

"Like a story!" The witch brightened.

"Only you see, one of the tasks . . ." Here Meg paused.

"Speak up, girl!"

"One of the tasks is to defeat you."

"Me?" The witch looked confused. "I have no quarrel with anyone."

"They want you out of this wood. Gone," Meg told her.

"Who does?" the old woman said crossly.

"My—the king. Only mostly, I think, it's the prime minister. It's his sort of idea. 'Timber and tract housing,' he said."

"I see." The witch stumped toward the front of the cottage.

Meg followed her. "Um . . ."

The witch spun around. "And who are you, missy?"

"I work at the castle. I heard about it up there."

"I suppose you want a reward for your bad news."

"Oh no," Meg said.

"Well then, be off!" The witch stepped onto her tiny porch.

This wasn't exactly what Meg had expected. She reminded herself of her mission. She was here to stop the princes, and to save the witch. "Don't you think—can I help you?" Meg ventured.

The witch seemed startled, but only for a moment. "I'm a witch, aren't I?" she said, stepping into her cottage and slamming the door behind her.

Feeling a little hurt, Meg went back the way she had come. The moors were too far to reach in half a day, at least on foot. And she had promised Cam she'd go up to the Dragon Crags with him tomorrow morning. Meg tromped through the woods, muttering to herself about ungrateful witches.

In the end, she went north through the woods and across the hill to the frog pond. Meg spent the rest of the afternoon catching dragonflies, having lost her taste for catching frogs at the witch's cottage. It was peaceful. It was a lovely change from the tower. But it was very quiet. Meg wished Cam or Dilly could have come along. She shared her picnic with the ducks and considered strategies for rescuing a possibly princess-eating dragon.

5

ATE IN THE DAY, MEG WENT INTO THE EDGE OF the woods to walk back to her tower. The sight of it still made her shudder, even though she reminded herself she had a way in and out.

"There you are!" Nort said when she came cautiously around the tower wall. "I was getting worried!"

"I spied on the princes and talked to the witch," Meg said. She had to tell somebody, and Nort was the only person around.

"Hurry and climb up," he fussed.

"Don't you want to hear about it?" Meg asked.

Nort looked surprised and pleased. "Of course. But Arbel will be here any minute. Can't you tell me from your window?"

"All right." Meg grabbed for the rope and began trying to haul herself up the tower. Instead, she slipped and fell back. Nort snorted.

"I'd like to see you try!" she told him.

"Watch," he said, taking hold of the rope. "You have to plant your feet against the wall and sort of walk on it." Nort demonstrated.

"Oh." Meg waited for him to come down and then tried again. It wasn't easy. When her toe slipped, she scraped her knee and dangled, but eventually she caught her footing and slowly made her way upward, until finally she clambered over the ledge into the tower room. Meg pulled the rope through the window, wishing she were still at the pond, at the witch's cottage, even in the castle—anywhere but here.

"Well?" Nort called.

Tomorrow Meg would be free once more, searching for the dragon with Cam. And, Meg promised herself, no matter what any of them said, this was the last night she would spend in the tower. Having caught her breath from the climb, she leaned on the window ledge to tell Nort the Short about her day.

The next morning dawned clear. The sun shining down on the gathered princes picked out heraldic devices sewn in threads of gold and silver. King Stromgard and Queen Istilda sat on a dais, with Garald beside them. The courtiers were clustered up front on actual chairs borrowed from the second-best dining room. Most of the guards and castle servants milled about behind them, and at least three hundred townspeople had turned out from Crown. A smiling farmwife was selling caramels, and a chubby boy was vending ballad lyrics about a prince who wasn't even in the contest.

Nort had really wanted to be there. It was with some difficulty that the others had persuaded him to stay and watch the empty tower. Today Dilly had brought Meg a wide straw hat, but Dilly was still jumpy. "That's one of the guards! He'll see you!" she told Meg, scooting into the man's line of sight.

"Will you stop *worrying*?"

"Even if someone sees her, they'll think she looks familiar, that's all," Cam reassured Dilly. Meg stroked her cotton skirt, pleased at how easily she could go from one world to another.

"You're right." Dilly stared up at the dais where the queen sat, fresh and fragile as a poppy. "You know," she said to Meg, "your mother would have been just the type to pine romantically in a tower. Or that frilly cousin of yours, Sonilia."

"She married a duke," Meg informed Cam.

Cam was watching the princes. "The prime minister went around collecting the entry fees last night," Cam said.

"Entry fees?" Meg asked, startled.

Cam nodded. "He seemed awfully happy about it."

A trumpet blared. A baby wailed. Everyone turned their eyes to the dais, cheering as King Stromgard stepped forward. The king proclaimed, "I welcome you all on this historic day—noble contestants, members of the royal court, good people of Crown, and other guests. My prime minister will now set forth the rules of the contest."

Meg felt an odd twinge, standing with the crowd as if her mother and father were strangers. Just then Garald moved to the king's side, bearing a scroll. Meg made a face, distracted from her feelings.

The prime minister's voice sounded thin after the king's rich tones. "Be it known that the one who will be named Champion of Greeve must slay the dragon and bring back its treasure to enrich our kingdom, rid our wood of the most foul witch, and capture the notorious bandit Rodolfo and his men. Lastly, *after* said prince has completed these three tasks"—Garald looked around sternly—"if he can carefully bring the Princess Margaret down from her tower, he will win the prize: half the kingdom and the princess's hand in marriage."

People began to shout, but Garald held up his hands, and they stilled. "Fair play and full proofs required, mind you," he added.

Then the king stood forth again to bellow, "Let the contest begin!" Everyone applauded and yelled. Dozens of princes ran to mount their horses and charge off. One of them even sounded a hunting horn. The crowd wandered about gossiping, dispersing into the castle and the town.

Meg and Cam and Dilly watched them leave.

"Who do you think will win?" a woman behind them asked someone.

"That Vantor is a goodly fellow," another woman replied.

"Prince Vain-tor," Meg whispered to her friends. "Let's go before my mother sees us."

Up on the dais, the king trailed after the queen. "Still not speaking, love?" he asked her.

She swished away toward the castle.

"Women don't always understand matters of politics," the prime minister remarked.

"Hold your tongue, Garald!" the king snarled.

"Sorry, Your Majesty."

The two men walked after the queen in silence. Finally the king looked at his minister. "You really think this is going to work? This—economic development thing?"

"As you so brilliantly phrased it, Sire, we'll 'clean out the bad and make room for the good.' "

"I said that?"

"Indeed," Garald answered quickly.

"Room for good gold, that is," the king muttered.

"The very best gold, Sire."

Prince Vantor paced to and fro in his tent, lifting the flap every so often to look out.

At last he caught sight of Horace walking toward him very slowly, half supporting an elderly peasant.

The prince let the tent flap fall and threw himself into an ornate camp chair. "The others will have captured the witch before we even make a start!" he growled when the two men entered.

Horace shook his head. "No. I've heard some pretty stories about the witch."

"She be a fair good hand wi' frogs," the old man said.

"No one asked you to speak," Vantor told him coldly.

"This is our guide," Horace explained. "Orl says he can take us right to the dragon's lair."

"Not right to," Orl said, shivering with fear or simply age. "Near enough to point at."

"That will do, won't it?" Horace said.

Vantor frowned. "This man is going to lead us up a mountain? He can hardly walk!"

"I'll get some of the men to carry him," Horace told his master.

The prince considered. "Very well. I want to leave before noon."

"Now," said Meg, leading her friends away from the field, "we're going after the dragon."

"Shouldn't we search for the bandits first?" Cam asked uneasily.

"Tomorrow."

"Are you sure the witch is all right?" Dilly put in. Meg had told them about the witch when they met up that morning.

"She said she didn't need help, but I'm still worried."

"I can go check up on her," Dilly said. "Do you two have any idea where to find the dragon?"

A prince on a chestnut charger galloped up behind them, and they all jumped out of the way.

"Tob told me which trail to take," said Cam. "I asked him the other day, and he said he went dragon-hunting once and got all the hair on the back of his head singed right off."

"Tob's old," Dilly objected.

"It was a long time ago."

"Maybe the dragon has moved its lair."

"Not far," Cam said, giving Meg a look. "They like to stay within range of castles."

"Where the princess-hunting is good?" Meg asked with false politeness.

Dilly smirked. "I'll be off, then. I won't miss you two very much if you're going to squabble."

"Squabble?" Cam said innocently as Dilly left.

"Just show me the way to the dragon," Meg told him.

She followed Cam past the visitors' tents. With all of the princes out after the dragon and the witch, the encampment was strangely quiet. A few servants sat playing cards.

"Now, we follow the king's road northwest for about a mile, and we should see a faint trail leading off east up the mountain," Cam said.

"Isn't there more than one trail?"

"Yes, but this is the first, and it's the right one."

Meg tugged at her hat. "I'm not wearing this thing all day."

"Hide it under a bush," Cam suggested.

"Hmmph," said Meg, tromping up the hill.

❧

With a hey and a hi and a ho! Prince Dagle sang tenor and Prince Dorn sang bass, somehow managing to hike up a mountain at the same time. They had gone along the king's road and up the most promising-looking trail. Any moment now, they might see a plume of evil smoke or a pile of bones, the marks of a dragon's lair.

Instead they saw a lot of rocks and some pine trees, then still more rocks and pine trees, also dirt. An eagle cried, soaring overhead.

"Wait!" Dagle said, and the brothers stopped. "Here, dragon, dragon, dragon!" Dagle called.

Dorn laughed. "He won't answer to that."

"Why not?"

"It's not his name!"

"How do you know?" Dagle asked.

"Because dragons have great, mythic names like Deathbreath and Snotfire," Dorn said knowingly.

"Ah. You're right."

They walked on in silence.

"This is probably the wrong mountain anyway," Dorn said suddenly.

Dagle looked amazed. "It could very well be the wrong mountain, brother! What shall we do?"

"We need information."

Dagle began to smile. "I know just where to find it."

"Where?"

"Why, in an alehouse! There we will find not only

good ale but some sturdy townsman who knows these parts and can tell us where to hunt out the beast!"

Cheered, the brothers turned about and set off down the slope for Crown.

The witch sat in an overstuffed flowered armchair reading a book with a scarlet cover depicting a golden-haired maiden being rescued by a very brawny young man in armor. Gorba shook her head as she reached page 147. "No, Esmeralda, his love is true!"

A sleepy voice croaked as if to answer her. Then, a great crashing of underbrush could be heard in the distance. A few of the frogs jumped, alarmed, but Gorba was absorbed in her book. One of the more timid frogs crept beneath the sofa.

Outside, Dilly slipped behind a stand of saplings, glad she hadn't worn her brightest dress.

The sound became louder. Someone was muttering in front of the cottage. Just as Gorba frowned, looking up from her novel, a voice was heard without. "Madam witch!" it cried. "Come forth and face your fate!"

Gorba sighed, sliding down a little in her chair. She tried holding the book closer to her nose.

Whoever it was pounded madly on the door. "Ho, witch!"

"Go away!" Gorba yelled.

After a moment's silence, the voice spoke again, even louder. "Come out, witch! Dare to meet the wrath of Prince George the Fourth of Shervelhame!"

Gorba rolled her eyes. The frogs croaked sympathet-ically. The witch put down the book, stalked to the door, and flung it open.

Her visitor, a little red-haired prince, glowered. Be-hind him, a dozen other princes jostled for a good view, nearly filling the little clearing.

"In the name of good King Stromgard of Greeve," the prince proclaimed, "I command you, evil crone, to depart from this place and trouble the kingdom no more!" The other princes stepped closer, sensing vic-tory.

"This is your last warning, you pack of royal idiots," Gorba said. "If you don't go away, I'll turn the lot of you into frogs!" She plucked Howie from her pocket. "Like this!"

"We fear not your magic!" a bearded prince called.

"You got that at the pond," another prince jeered.

"Fine," Gorba snapped. *"Hexibus, tantalus, langulus, trab—"*

"To me!" George yelled, lunging at the witch. The rest of the bunch followed, piling onto the porch in a tangle of arms and legs, nearly drowning out the witch's voice. The tangle shrank and turned green. A couple of men-at-arms scrambled to their feet and ran.

Gorba sat up to catch her breath. She patted her hair back into place. "I gave 'em fair warning, didn't I?" A chorus of voices from within the cottage croaked their agreement as a cranky witch began shooing frogs into the house.

6

T THE EDGE OF THE CLEARING, PRINCE BAIN stepped out, one of his men beside him. "Now, *that* was a good trick," he said genially.

"What are we going to do about her?" the other man asked.

"Fight fire with fire," Bain told him. "We need some magic of our own."

Just then Dilly's fingers slipped. The branch she was holding scratched across its neighbor. Dilly stilled it quickly, but the voices stopped. She stood up partway and tried to move away from the cottage at a crouch. She hadn't gotten very far when she heard running feet and felt a hand on her shoulder.

"What are you doing here?" a rough voice asked as the man spun her around. "Spying?"

Dilly couldn't think what to say. But the other man said, "Let go of her, Feg. I'm sure she'll be happy to explain herself."

Reluctantly, the prince's companion loosed his grip on her shoulder, and Dilly stepped back. The prince was smiling at her, his eyes glinting green. "I am Prince Bain. Who are you?"

"Dilly, my lord," she managed to say. He didn't look easy to fool.

"Why are you here?"

Suddenly Dilly knew exactly why someone like herself would be at the witch's cottage. "Oh, sir," she said, "I can't tell a gentleman." She threw in a nervous giggle.

The two men glanced at each other. "Were you hoping to see the witch?" the prince asked.

Dilly nodded. "I work up at the castle, and there's this boy, he works there, too, and they say the witch, they say she knows about such things." Dilly batted her eyelashes a bit.

"She's after a love spell?" Feg asked dubiously.

"It would appear so," Bain replied. "And you hid because?"

"Oh," Dilly said, blushing, "I got here, and I saw all these princes about, coming after the witch, so I thought if I just waited—" She shut her mouth abruptly.

Prince Bain laughed. "The old woman would turn us into frogs, and you could get on with your business?"

Dilly's eyes widened. "I'd never wish such a thing on a gentleman!" she protested.

"Of course not," said Feg, still suspicious.

"Run along, girl," Prince Bain told her. "The witch is busy with other guests."

"Thank you, Your Highness," Dilly said. There was no need to fake her relief as she took to her heels. It was a pity she'd have to wait all day to tell Meg what this prince was planning for the witch.

Meg and Cam watched a group of men struggling up the slope far, far below. "I'll bet it's Vantor," Meg said. "They're wearing gray, like his tent."

Cam coughed, waving away a puff of smoke that swirled past lazily, as if a giant were smoking his great pipe in the cave beside them.

"We've got to go in *now*, before they get here!" Meg whispered furiously.

"And if the dragon eats you?" Cam asked.

"You're chicken!" Meg challenged.

"No. I just think we should let it kill that fathead Vantor, and *then* decide what to do!"

"What if that fathead kills it first?"

Cam didn't seem too concerned.

"And takes the treasure?"

Cam shrugged.

"I'm going in whether you come or not," Meg announced.

"They *like* princesses!" Cam exclaimed. *"Flame-broiled!"*

She looked at him narrowly. "Fine. I'll let you go first."

"Meg . . ."

But the princess had scrambled up and was clambering over the rocks to the cave's mouth. Cam had no choice. "As usual," he muttered, following her into the darkness. He coughed again as another twirl of dragon smoke wafted up his nose.

"Come *on*," Meg said, lowering her voice.

Cam stepped past her. A rock caught his shoulder. He moved away from the cave wall with a grunt. "Take my hand," he said. Meg didn't argue for once, just reached out to grab his hand with hers. They stepped forward, bumping along through the darkening tunnel. Gravel slid beneath their feet. Cam slipped once, but Meg pulled him up.

After a while they came to a fork. They touched the walls, stumbling back and forth. "This way," Cam said finally.

"How do you know?"

"It smells of smoke."

The two walked down the new tunnel. Meg could feel her heart beating faster, and Cam had forgotten all about the prince behind them. They had to choose their way at two more points. In one place, the cave branched in three different directions. And then suddenly they emerged into the dragon's chamber.

Cam and Meg stopped. The high hall of the dragon was lit an eerie red-gold. They stared about, startled enough to be easy prey for a moment. The room was filled with treasure, centuries' worth of collecting by an oversize pack rat with very good taste. Golden chalices and goblets and coins, emeralds and rubies and pearls, several suits of armor with—Meg gulped—

fragments of bone sticking out of them. Half a skull grinned crookedly atop an inlaid chest. A swirl of satin looked uncomfortably like one of the dresses tossed on Meg's bedroom floor.

"Where's the dragon?" Cam breathed an inch from Meg's ear.

Meg peered higher and deeper into the cavern. Stones were piled around the edges, and . . . "Over there," she murmured, pointing. "Those aren't stones." In the farthest shadows, like a jumble of great swords and spears made of silver and pearl, lay the vast skeleton of a dragon. A tatter of wing silk like another lady's gown hung down from one long, arching bone.

"It's dead," Cam said, his voice ringing out with his surprise.

"Shh. Yes, but if it's dead, where is the smoke coming from?"

Cam turned around. "And the light, for that matter."

"Look," Meg said, pointing again. Beyond the highest pile of treasure, the red glow was stronger.

They tried to close in quietly, but their feet clinked and clanked, stepping over and around the dragon's gold.

Something hissed like a large teakettle. Meg stopped as the glow was dimmed by a new gust of smoke. She moved forward, more slowly now. She gestured to Cam. He nodded and worked his way around the side of the pile of jewels and coins and armor as she began to scale the miniature golden mountain.

Meg lifted her eyes over the top. An instant later, Cam appeared below Meg, to her right. The dragon squawked.

"It's a baby," Meg cooed.

The dragon was just smaller than one of her father's wolfhounds. Its wings and throat were butter-colored, its back was scarlet streaked with amber, its staring eyes were round and black, with gold slits. It glowed like a hearth fire at midwinter.

"Stay back," Cam said. "Just because it's young doesn't mean it isn't dangerous."

The dragon breathed out. Little flames licked the nearest coins, melting them atop a glob of already blurry gold.

"It's beautiful," Meg said. "You see?"

"See what?"

"We can't let them kill it!"

Cam sighed. "I hope you have a plan."

"It's just— What was *that*?"

But they both knew, hearing the voices and footsteps outside. Prince Vantor was already here.

"Another ale!" Dagle called. The barkeep obliged.

"Wonderful stuff," Dorn said. "Do you know where we might find the dragon?"

The men at the nearest table looked around. The customers of Ye Broken Egg appeared to be mostly farmers, but here and there a flash of velvet shone amid the homespun.

"No," the man replied. "Sorry, good sirs." He turned as if to go, then hesitated. "If any of this lot has the information you need, he'll be most likely to assist you when his throat is wet."

"Wet throat?" Dagle repeated.

"He means buy them ale," Dorn whispered loudly.

Still more men were watching the twin princes now. Dagle smiled back at them. "I'm buying," he announced, "for the man who can tell us about the dragon."

A dozen chairs scooted in their direction. A dozen voices began talking at once. "Here, my granddad saw the creature with his own eyes!" cried a peasant.

"Your granddad's long dead!" another burst out. "My father, now, he knows the exact cave—"

"The thing only eats young girls, so you best bring one of those along for bait!" said a farmer with a grim chuckle.

Dagle laughed, pleased. "One at a time, good sirs. Barkeep, bring us a round of drinks!" The men around them cheered.

It was well past noon when the brothers emerged into the street, their pockets lighter along with their hearts. "That went well," Dorn told his brother.

Dagle frowned, striding back through the city of Crown. "But if it has six heads and can smell a mouse at a distance of two miles, how do we kill it?"

"Dagle," his twin exclaimed, "we have to trick the creature!"

"How?" Dagle neatly sidestepped a bit of gutter muck.

Dorn thought for a mere four blocks before he came up with the answer. When he did, he stopped and put his hands on his brother's shoulders. "We, the twin princes of Hanaby Keep, are going to build a dragon trap," he proclaimed.

Dagle's eyes lit up. "That's fantastic! And we'll bait it with—well, not the princess."

"No," Dorn said regretfully. "I've heard they like a juicy cow nearly as much, though," he added.

"So the first thing we need is a cow," Dagle mused. He looked around and soon spotted a small boy. "You there!" The boy came closer. "Where can we get a cow in these parts?"

The boy hitched up his scruffy britches. "My granny has a cow."

"Well then," Dorn said, holding out a coin, "take us to your granny!"

"Dorn, what about those other princes?" Dagle said when they were on their way to the cow by means of a series of winding streets.

"You're not worried, are you?" Dorn asked, astonished.

"I don't want them getting to the beast first, is all."

"I do."

Dagle blinked. "Whatever for?"

"So the dragon can eat them."

Dagle laughed, and Dorn laughed with him, till the small boy faltered and Dagle had to wave another coin to get him moving.

"So that's how we narrow the competition," Dagle said, snorting.

Dorn guffawed. "*What* competition?"

Prince Vantor held the torch high, his eyes burning amber in the reflected light of the dragon's treasure.

Horace waited behind him. "What do you see?" he asked finally. Vantor moved forward as if in a dream, and his manservant came after him. They stood silently gawking at the chamber.

Meg lay still behind a large suit of armor, trying not to touch the neck bone jutting out of it at a horrible angle just next to her head. The little dragon purred nearby. Cam twitched in his hiding place, making a coin slide.

"What was that?" Horace said, breaking the golden spell.

Vantor gestured at the great skeleton. "Dragon's dead."

"And you killed it," Horace said wisely.

Vantor smiled. "Of course." He stooped to fill his hands with jewels.

"But the smoke," his servant began.

"Go find out," the prince told him, not taking his eyes from the gems.

Horace tramped toward the back of the chamber, around the hill of gold. He stopped short. "Dragon!" he said. Then he laughed.

Vantor let the jewels drop, running to join his servant. "Ha!" he said. "You see, Horace? I'll slay a dragon after all!" The little dragon hissed at him.

"Sword or spear?"

"Not much sport," the prince replied. "First let's start moving the treasure. I don't want dragon's blood all over my gold."

"And the king's share?" Horace asked.

"Pity," Vantor told him, "but the dragon had a very poor hoard. A goblet, a small chest filled with coins, a few inferior gems."

"A pity indeed."

Meg nearly jumped up yelling at these words of treachery.

"Go and get the others while I fetch a few of those dragon bones to make it look good," the prince said.

"And Orl?"

"Who?"

"The old man. Our guide."

"He found his way up the mountain. Let him find his way down."

"Yes, my lord." Horace left the chamber.

If Meg tilted her head at an uncomfortable angle, she could just see Cam behind a moldering chest. After a few moments, she could hear Prince Vantor hacking away at the huge skeleton with his sword.

The little dragon chuffed oddly, climbing over a stack of coins. When it sneezed, flame shot toward the ceiling.

"I'll put that out soon enough," Vantor called

jovially. Meg didn't think he'd be very jovial if he found her there. Or Cam.

Horace soon came back with a group of Vantor's men, and the newcomers gasped at the sight of the treasure. Finally they were calm enough to listen to their leader's words of inspiration.

"Men," the prince said sonorously, "it's not that I doubt your loyalty, but I'll search every one of you when we're ready to go down the mountain and again when we set up camp. If I find so much as a single gold coin in your pocket, I'll cut your throat and leave your body for the wolves."

The men muttered.

"However," the prince continued, "do good work, and when this is all over I will reward each of you with a share of the treasure."

The men cheered cautiously.

Behind the chest, Cam rolled his eyes. Vantor didn't seem like the sharing type. Cam managed to look over at Meg. She made a face. Then her expression changed. Cam stopped smiling, too, remembering abruptly that Prince Vantor was seeking Meg's hand in marriage. Maybe the prince would just take the treasure and go home. It would be worth it to be rid of him.

7

OR THE NEXT HOUR, VANTOR'S MEN CAME IN and out of the cave at an alarming rate, carrying treasure away. If they keep going like this, they'll soon reach our side of the hoard, Meg thought. A moment later, she forgot about the men when the baby dragon came right up to her foot and breathed on it with its too-hot breath. *Stop that!* Meg thought. The dragon tasted her ankle with its forked tongue. She wondered with a shock if Cam was right, if the darling creature would open its spiky jaws and bite her foot right off. Meg lay tightly, willing the baby dragon to leave. *Go away!* she thought at it. With a cranky snuffle, the dragon moved off around the chamber.

"Hey, out of my way!" One of Vantor's men tried kicking the dragon and got his ankle burned for his trouble. Vantor only laughed.

Back and forth the men went, till Meg thought she might fall asleep and give herself away by rolling over.

But at last the prince's servants must have stopped to rest, since they didn't return. Instead, Vantor held a conference with Horace in the dragon's chamber. "We've got as much as we can carry," the servant said.

"We're not leaving any of this here!"

"We can make another trip tomorrow."

The prince said nothing.

"Or later tonight," Horace went on. "We'll post a guard."

"You stand guard. I don't trust the others."

And, mercifully, they left.

Meg and Cam waited a long while, but all was quiet except for the sound of the dragon baby creeping along like a great lizard. Meg lifted her head, then stood up. "Where did he go?" she whispered.

Cam stood up, too. "He'll be at the cave mouth."

Meg put her hands on her hips. "We've got to get out," she said, "and we're taking the dragon with us."

Nort shifted about anxiously as the sun dropped lower and lower. Where was the princess? Arbel might be a bit dim, but he would certainly notice a rope hanging down from the tower window.

Someone was moving toward him from the castle. Nort frantically cast about for a convincing story to tell the older guard, but when the figure came closer he saw that it was Dilly. Nort leaned his spear against the wall and hurried forward to meet her.

"Well?" she said, looking up at the tower with

its dark window. "I've got to tell her about the witch."

Nort shook his head. "I don't know where she is, and Arbel will be here any minute." His face lit up. "But you can go up! This is definitely an emergency!"

Dilly backed away. "No it isn't!"

"Dilly!"

Her face whitened. "I can't, Nort. I want to help, truly, but I can't."

"Why not?"

Dilly bit her lip. "Promise you won't laugh?" She couldn't believe she was confiding in Nort the Creep.

"I promise." Nort actually sounded kind.

Dilly steeled herself. "I'm afraid of heights."

"Oh." Nort looked surprised, but he didn't laugh. He didn't seem to understand, either. "Dilly, you have to. Arbel will see the rope."

"Not just a little afraid," Dilly cried. "I'll fall!"

She could tell Nort was starting to believe her. "We've got to do *something*," he said.

Dilly thought. "We could tell him—we could say . . ." She closed her mouth.

"I've tried all day to think of a good reason for a rope to be hanging out Meg's window, and I haven't come up with a single thing," Nort said, shaking his head.

Then Dilly smiled. "I know."

"What?"

"You can climb up there."

"Me?" Nort yelped. "I'm not a princess!"

"Neither am I," Dilly pointed out. "You don't have to talk."

"Arbel would wonder where I was," Nort said unwillingly.

"I'll cover for you down here." Dilly paused. "Please?" she added, flushing.

Nort grinned suddenly. "Clever Dilly, are you asking for a favor?"

She snorted. "It's for the princess, and you know it."

He waited.

"Yes!" Dilly said. "Now go!"

"All right," Nort told her sweetly. He climbed up the rope faster than Dilly would have thought possible.

A moment later, the rope slid upward. A candle flared high in the tower. Not ten minutes after that, Arbel came tramping across the meadow.

"What's this, then?" he said, bewildered. "Young Dilly?"

Dilly nodded. "Oh, sir," she said, going all wide-eyed for the second time in one day, "they needed Nort back at the castle. They said you'd be here any minute, so it would be all right."

Arbel frowned. "And who might 'they' be?"

"Why, Hanak," Dilly told him.

Bain shifted, crouching behind the rocks near the dragon's cave. At first he had been puzzled. Smoke still blew out of the cave, but there was no sign of a battle.

Dragons usually managed to kill a few of a prince's men-at-arms, if not the prince himself. Perhaps the dragon had been dead for some time, and the fire was man-made. Vantor's men had been hauling treasure out of the cave for at least an hour. A live dragon wouldn't have put up with that.

When the men brought out a clutch of long, dry bones, Bain knew he was right. Vantor hadn't had to fight a dragon at all. And, Bain realized, Greeve hadn't even known its dragon was dead. Bain chuckled softly to himself.

Then he watched Vantor stride out of the cave behind the men, leaving his most trusted servant just inside. Prince Bain smiled. Golden Vantor was stealing the dragon's golden hoard. Bain could tell by the way Vantor's men had been peering about, as if they were expecting the other princes to show up and catch them at it.

Other than Bain himself, this was highly unlikely, since Bain had managed to send most of the remaining princes off into the mountains some miles west of here with a few carefully dropped words. As for Vantor, it obviously didn't occur to him to worry. The man expected fortune to favor him as a matter of course. Bain sat back to wait. He was very well acquainted with good fortune.

The baby dragon still glowed, but it hadn't burned anything for quite a while. "It's been living on rabbits," Cam said.

Meg stepped forward to see the small bones. "And bats."

"But this beast isn't our biggest problem. Our biggest problem is Vantor's guard."

The dragon came over to lick Meg's leg. "Stop that!" she said.

"I told you they like princesses," Cam had to say. Meg chose to ignore him as the dragon snortled off again.

"Maybe there's another way out," Meg said.

Cam started to shake his head, then stopped. "A dragon's a clever beast," he said. "Not you," he told the baby dragon as it crashed into his legs and veered away, shaking its head. "But a full-grown female wouldn't have a nursery without a bolt-hole. The problem is finding it. We don't have a torch."

"We've got a dragon," Meg said. "It glows."

Cam looked dubiously at the creature. "That's true."

Meg headed toward the arched doorway. "Bring that cloak."

"What for?"

"In case we need to cover the dragon with it."

Cam didn't point out that one breath from the dragon would turn the ancient velvet to cinders. He simply grabbed the thing.

Meg set about coaxing the dragon out of the chamber. "And some treasure—from the far wall, where they won't notice," she said.

"What for?" Cam asked again.

"For when it's homesick!" Meg stroked the dragon's

nose. "I'll take some, too," she said, her expression suddenly ominous. "For proof." Meg and Cam quickly filled their pockets with jewels and coins.

The dragon had wandered off once more. "Come on, sweetie," Meg told it. The dragon snuffled after her. Cam followed them, the cloak over his arm.

Out in the passageway, Meg and Cam retraced their steps to the nearest fork and began sending the baby dragon down various passages, hoping its fondness for rabbits would lead them to another exit.

The plan didn't work. But something else happened. Horace heard the noise and came back into the cave, running toward the treasure chamber. He gave an angry yell. Then Horace started trying the passageways himself.

Meg snatched the cloak from Cam and crouched to put it over the dragon, trying to hide its light. "Can't you stop glowing?" she asked it.

To Meg's astonishment, the dragon gave her a reproachful black-and-gold look and dimmed considerably. "It understands me!" she told Cam.

"Never mind that. This is our chance!"

"What?"

"Horace went into the next tunnel over. The long, twisty one."

"Let's go, dragon!" Meg said. She hurried back up the tunnel after Cam, with the dragon trundling along beside her.

But just as they reached the main passage, they heard

a burst of footsteps and crashed right into Horace, whose lantern went flying. Horace grabbed at them, astonished. Cam had fallen down, and he squawked as Horace stepped on him. "Who are you?" Horace demanded harshly.

Cam crawled out from under. Horace caught Meg by the shoulder. She tried to twist away, but his grip was too strong. If they only had . . . Meg thought of the dragon. *Fire!* she willed him frantically, hoping for the best. The dragon, who was glowing again, belched. Flame splashed across Horace's back and shoulders. He let go of Meg, yelling in pain.

Meg slapped the sparks that had caught her own hair as she turned to run. *Come on!* Meg thought fiercely, and the dragon came after her, with Cam right behind.

Down the mountainside, Prince Vantor's horse strained and danced. After waiting for him all afternoon, the stallion was eager to race down the hill. "Can't you go any faster?" the prince snarled at his men.

"The treasure is heavy," a scar-faced guardsman pointed out. "Unless you want to ride on ahead?"

"Don't be a fool," Vantor snapped. His temper cooled quickly, though. Ten men, each pair carrying a chest filled with treasure—he could buy a small kingdom with that much, and a large one with the entire trove. The long bones the eleventh man dragged would win him half of this very kingdom, a half easily doubled. Vantor smiled, spurring his horse. For a heedless moment or two, the prince gave the animal his head. But he reined in his mount abruptly when he came to a barrier across the path. Rubble and sticks, felled saplings—there were too many owls calling in the twilight.

"To arms!" Vantor shouted, spinning back up the trail. His men quickly dropped the chests to draw their swords, but the road was suddenly full of bandits, more than a dozen of them, and one of Vantor's men was already down with an arrow in his shoulder.

"No!" Vantor howled, striking out with his sword. He fought like a dragon himself, guarding his hoard, but all too soon his men were surrounded, their weapons scattered, one of them dead and two more injured. Five bandits rushed the prince. When it was over, Vantor stood weaponless and glaring.

One of the bandits laughed, and Vantor knew, despite her hood and the dark scarf covering her mouth and nose. "A woman?" Vantor said, outraged. "What are you after?"

"We'll take those chests you've got," she called merrily. "Thank you *ever* so much for slaying the dragon."

The bandits tied Vantor and his men up hand and foot. They packed the treasure on their horses—and Vantor's. Then they left, but not before the bandit leader had slipped a single gold coin into Vantor's pocket. "A souvenir," she said. "Maybe we'll send someone to look for you in the morning." With that she pulled out a knife. Vantor's eyes darkened, but she merely reached to cut off a lock of his shining hair. "A fair trade, don't you think?" she asked. Vantor could only grit his teeth as the bandits disappeared down the slope with his beautiful gold.

Farther up the mountain, Bain watched with interest as a boy and a girl raced out of the cave, a baby dragon at their heels. Now they lunged for cover. "There *was* a dragon!" he said. "Or half a dragon." Bain thought of catching up with them and taking the dragon, but he had more important matters to attend to. "Later," he said amiably.

Bain slipped into the cave. With his charcoal cloak and fog-colored britches, Prince Bain resembled the rocky walls just inside the cave. He hid in a deep alcove and readied his cloak. A moment later Vantor's man thundered toward the mouth of the cave, looking rather singed. Prince Bain stepped out behind the man. In one swift move Bain wrapped the cloak about his head and arms. Horace struggled. "Do you want me to hit you with a rock?" the prince asked, pulling back on Horace's elbows.

Vantor's servant stopped fighting, his body tense.

"That's better," Bain told him. He tied the man's hands and feet and settled Horace just outside the cave. "Don't go rolling off the mountain," the prince advised. Horace's curse was muffled by the cloak. Bain scoured about to find a fallen tree branch and lit it with a flint from his pocket. He went into the cave with his make-shift torch, coming across Horace's fallen lantern at the mouth of a side passage. "You see?" Bain said softly. "Good fortune." He lit the lantern and walked deeper into the cave.

8

ELL?" THE KING PUT HIS FEET UP ON AN EM-
broidered footstool and settled back to listen.

"I've spoken to the remaining princes," the prime minister told him.

" 'Remaining'? What's happened?"

Garald cleared his throat. "It appears the witch cast a spell on a number of our candidates."

"Hmmph," the king said. "Frogs, I imagine?"

The prime minister nodded. "Most of the others spent all day searching for the dragon's cave."

"None of them found it?" the king asked incredulously.

"Not that I've heard."

"Go on."

"Prince Vantor hasn't returned yet. Perhaps he's found the dragon and is on his way here even now—he seemed a likely sort," Garald said hopefully.

"Perhaps the dragon found *him*." The king chortled. "And?"

"That's about all. Those twin princes were last seen in a tavern. Bought everybody drinks, wanting to talk about the dragon."

"There was a prince from the north, the one with all the fur," the king mused.

"Frog."

"And the short one with the red hair?"

"Frog."

"What about the dark-haired lad? Bain, isn't it?"

Garald shook his head. "He's still off somewhere."

The king creaked forward. "I want results, Garald. You do know that."

"Yes, Your Majesty. Just give them a few more days!"

"Not them. You. I'll give *you* a few more days to sort out this mess." The king pursed his lips, making his beard bristle. "I don't think the neighbors will like hearing that their sons have been changed into amphibians."

"No, Your Majesty," Garald said faintly.

King Stromgard went to the window and forced himself to look across the meadow at the tower, where candlelight illuminated the high window. "Do you suppose she's all right up there?"

"It should be a pleasant interlude for her," Garald reassured his monarch. "She gets the very same food that you and the queen eat. She also has plenty of books, embroidery, and a fine view of the castle."

"Let's get this thing over with," the king said, turning back to the prime minister.

"Yes, Sire. Will you excuse me?"

"Go on," King Stromgard told him. "And send me my minstrel on your way out. I could use some cheering up."

The prime minister practically ran to the door, but he couldn't avoid the king's last words. "Results, Garald!"

Nort paced the tower room, careful to stay well away from the window. If Arbel caught sight of him! Nort sighed, staring around the room. No wonder the princess wanted out. He sat down gingerly at the table. The books were all about royal girl stuff. Maybe the wedding one would be good for a laugh. Nort flipped through it. Gowns and geegaws and—he found a wedding where the bride was kidnapped by a rival monarch. The wedding turned into a great bloody war. Nort forgot where he was, turning pages as the candle burned low.

"We can't take that creature to the castle," Cam argued. They had stopped well away from the cave, perching on a heap of rocks beside a dark stand of pines.

"We have to tell my father about Vantor!" Meg cried. "The dragon's our proof!"

"I thought you wanted to save it."

Meg crossed her arms over her knees. The dragon leaned against her, thrumming like an oversize cat. "Of course!"

"What do you think your father would do to it?" Cam asked reasonably.

"Oh."

"What's more—" Cam started. He stopped himself.

"What? What's more what?" she demanded.

Cam sighed. "He's not going to believe anything you say right now. You're not one of his wonderful princes, and you're not in that tower where you're supposed to be."

"He'll say I'm just trying to ruin things, won't he?" Meg said glumly.

Cam was silhouetted against the starry sky, but she could see his nod. "Probably."

Meg gasped.

"What?" Cam asked, alarmed.

"I'm supposed to be in the tower right now!" Not that she wanted to go back, of course, but Nort would be waiting for her.

"Well, either everybody knows . . ."

"Or Nort's thought of something." They fell silent, pondering this unlikely possibility. Meg put her arm around the dragon.

"Doesn't that burn?" Cam asked.

"No. I told him not to. I asked him not to burn anything unless I said so."

"He?" Cam repeated. "What makes you think it's a boy dragon?"

Meg stroked the dragon's head. "I just know." She could feel a sort of something—agreement, maybe, when she guessed right about the dragon. "It's like he's talking to me."

"Uh-huh," Cam said, unconvinced.

Meg began considering the dragon's possibilities. "He'd make a good bed warmer. He could start the fire in the mornings. He could be taught to catch rats."

"My sister loves cats," Cam said in a thoughtful voice.

"That's it, then," Meg said.

Moving the dragon wasn't easy. He seemed happy to follow Meg, but he was like a large puppy, bumbling off on side trips every two minutes, so that she had to keep calling him back.

Cam's sister lived on the other side of the Witch's Wood. They followed a goat track leading east. "If this doesn't turn south, we can make our own way down once we're past the wood," Cam explained.

"How will we know?" It was a clear night, but still dark enough that they stumbled every so often. Finally it occurred to Meg to ask the dragon to light up a bit. This meant they could see the way ahead about half the time, since the creature kept rambling off the trail, sniffing happily.

"I'm hoping we'll be able to see the lights of the farms in the valley once we've gone far enough."

"And if they've all gone to bed?"

"Then we keep going till we come to the moors and the bandits steal our dragon!" Cam snapped. "Do you have a better idea?"

Meg didn't. They tramped awhile in cranky silence.

Then Meg decided to forgive Cam by talking about something else. "He needs a name."

"Who?"

"The dragon."

"How about Sniffy?" Cam suggested.

"Cam!"

"What? There he goes, sniffing and sniffing—"

"No." Meg caught herself from falling again. "He needs a name he can grow into. Something dramatic."

"Nosy?"

"I'll think of a name by myself, thank you very much," she huffed.

"I hope Tob doesn't mess with my bean vines," Cam mused. "He was mad the other day when I went off spying with you."

"Don't talk about beans. Aren't you hungry?"

"I'm trying not to think about it," Cam said.

They walked on for at least another mile. "Stop!" Meg cried.

"What?"

"I do see a light!"

"Where?"

"Down there!" Meg called the dragon so she could get a better look at the terrain. Sure enough, a trail dropped away down the hill. They had missed it in the darkness.

Dagle and Dorn had to follow the little boy so far south of the city that they lost a fraction of their good humor by the time they got to his grandmother's house. When the child's granny agreed to sell the animal and invited them for supper besides, they soon cheered up again. Now they were heading back.

"Shouldn't we have reached the city by now?" Dorn asked.

"I think we missed the turn," Dagle told him, tugging on the cow's lead. "Maybe we should spend the night by the side of the road."

"Surely we're getting close."

They trudged along, their shadows swinging with the sweep of Dorn's lantern. The road began to narrow. Soon after, it sloped upward.

"What's that?" Dagle said.

Dorn shuttered the lantern briefly, peering ahead. "It's a light!"

They quickened their pace. But Dagle slowed again, disappointed. "That's not the city. It's another traveler. Maybe he's lost, like we are."

"Maybe he's not."

They came closer. "Ho there!" Dagle called.

"Hello?" came a girl's voice.

"It's a lass," Dorn told his brother.

"And a lad," Dagle said when they met up with the other travelers. A boy with curly brown hair stood beside a girl with her lighter hair in a braid. The girl stooped to adjust an odd-looking bundle at her feet—a dusty cloak that seemed to be moving about. There was no sign of a light.

The cow mooed uneasily.

"Why, it's the lad and lass from the castle," Dorn said.

"Hello," the boy said. "How are you?"

"Very well," Dagle said. "We've just purchased this fine cow!"

"What for?" the girl asked. She straightened and stepped in front of her bundle. The bundle coughed.

"Mind your manners, Emma," the boy said. "My sister's not used to princes," he explained.

The girl nearly choked, she was that abashed.

"I remember," Dagle said kindly.

"You see, lass, this cow is going to help us catch a dragon!" Dorn said.

The girl looked alarmed. "It is?"

Dagle smiled. "Don't be afraid for our safety, lass. The cow is merely bait for the ingenious trap that my brother and I will soon be constructing."

The boy put his foot out to one side as if it hurt. Something thumped.

"What's that you've got?" Dorn asked, lifting his lantern.

"My auntie's pig," the girl blurted. "We're taking him to her farm."

Dorn lowered the lantern. "You aren't lost, then?" he asked, pleased.

"No," said the boy. "Are you?"

Dagle and Dorn glanced at each other. "Well," Dagle said, "perhaps a little."

"Do you want the castle or the dragon cave?" the boy said, rushing things.

"Dragon cave?" Dagle asked, astonished. "You know where it is?"

The boy waved his hand behind him. "We just passed that way, but we're not princes, so it didn't interest us much."

"Of course not," Dorn said graciously. "Please go on."

"Follow this path up the mountain and you'll soon come to a goat track. After that it's due west, a good ways off."

Dagle dug in his pockets. "Here's a coin for your troubles. I'll give you another if you'll show us the cave!"

The girl shook her head.

"Sorry," the boy said. "We're in a hurry ourselves. Pig's hungry." The creature snorted as if to agree, then blundered off into the shadows beside the road.

The girl had been very quiet, sweet child. Now she spoke suddenly. "After you pass the dragon's cave, you'll see another trail leading down the mountain to the road. That will take you back to the castle."

"Thank you, lass!" Dorn tossed her a coin. She caught it with one hand, blushing bright red in the lantern light. "Farewell!" the princes said. They marched up the slope with their cow behind them. The lad and lass turned about to watch them go.

"I can't believe you said that!" Meg hissed.

"Said what?" Cam asked, starting down the path again.

" 'Not used to princes'!"

"Well, are you?"

"No," Meg had to admit.

The baby dragon reappeared. "Look, Meg," Cam said as they walked on. "Servants don't question princes without a lot of bowing and scraping, and I didn't think you remembered that."

"I'm supposed to be a servant," Meg conceded. She held up the coin. "No one's ever thrown money at me before!"

They both giggled. "Come on," Cam said. "We'll soon be at Hookhorn Farm."

"Why is it called that?"

"After my great-grandfather's prize bull."

It was nearly an hour later when, footsore and famished, they approached a tidy farmhouse. The dragon had fallen asleep and refused to wake up. They had been trying to carry him between them, wrapped in the cloak. It was slow going.

A horse whinnied, and a few chickens woke up, squawking as if a fox were about. "They smell the dragon," Meg said.

A light flared in the house. Cam stepped ahead of Meg to knock on the door.

"Who is it?" a woman's voice called.

"It's Cam."

The door opened. The woman inside had Cam's brown hair and sun-browned skin. "What are you doing here at this hour?" She stared beyond her brother. "Who's that?" She rubbed her eyes. "*What's* that?"

"This is the princess, and that's a baby dragon," Cam said cheerfully.

Dorn and Dagle led the cow along the trail. " 'Beautiful ba-da-di-ba,' " Dagle muttered. "No, not quite."

"What are you talking about?" Dorn asked.

"I'll tell you when I'm finished. 'Better than a horse'—no, 'better than . . .' "

"A cow?" Dorn suggested.

Dagle frowned, changing the subject. "Shouldn't we have come to the cave already? We've walked and walked."

Dorn looked around. "Maybe we passed it in the darkness." He clanged his lantern. "Pity the thing burned out."

"Shh!"

"What?" Dorn said.

"Don't you hear that?"

"The cow?"

Dagle cocked his head. "Sounds like someone shouting."

They quickened their pace. The cow, never having been this far from home in her life, had begun to balk. "Come on, you!" Dagle told her. The cow mooed with gusto and broke into a trot, apparently deciding the barn might lie just ahead, after all. She passed Dagle, then dragged him after her like a large dog on a lead.

"Wait!" Dorn said. The brothers ran down the hill. Dorn swerved sideways when he heard voices to the right of the trail, but Dagle had to slow the cow down and circle back.

"Who's that?" Dorn asked.

"Prince Vantor!" a hoarse voice replied.

"Help!" someone else cried, but the first voice muttered and all was silent.

Dagle led the cow up beside Dorn. "What are you doing down there?" he called, baffled.

"We tied ourselves up like this!" Vantor said furiously. *"Now untie us!"*

Dorn and his brother exchanged twin looks in the dim light of the moon. "You needn't be rude," Dorn said. "We're happy to help."

9

o!" JANNA PUT HER HANDS ON HER HIPS. "No, no, no, and no!"

"What if your princess begs you to?" Meg ventured.

"My princess is supposed to be at the top of a tower, swooning over the thought of all those princes."

Meg scowled. "Would you?"

"Would I what?"

"Swoon?"

"Sit down, you two," Janna said, laughing.

The kitchen was warm and friendly. Drying herbs scented the room. A modest fire lit the curves of copper pots and a handful of green-and-yellow teacups. The dragon explored this new place with interest. He discovered the cats. The cats discovered the rafters.

"You see?" Janna gestured. "He's a troublemaker."

"You didn't answer," Cam said.

"Swoon? No. I'm well past swooning. I might swoon

over the thought of a supper someone else cooked and a bed someone else made, mind you."

"You wouldn't like how they did it," Cam told her.

"There is that." Janna brought them a basket of biscuits. "Hungry?"

"Starving!" Meg cried. Her stomach did flip-flops at the sight of the food.

"You could have said," Janna scolded. She hurried to heat up a dish of chicken and noodles. The next few minutes were spent happily as Cam and Meg filled their empty bellies.

"I would tuck you both into bed," Janna said, "but I imagine your night's adventure isn't over."

"No," Cam said, yawning.

"Going to tell me about it?"

Cam looked at Meg. "I'm not sure."

"You'd better," Janna said. "After bringing a dragon into my kitchen!" She shook her head, still amazed.

"We're trying to stop those princes from bothering . . . certain citizens," Meg said.

"As in, the good people of Crown?" Janna asked. "Or perhaps you're referring to yourself."

"You *are* a citizen, Meg," Cam said, grinning.

"Couldn't you just keep him here for a few days?" Meg pleaded. "If you think at him very sternly, he'll do as he's told."

The dragon had curled up in a rumpled heap on the hearth. Janna regarded him warily as she began clearing the table. "Some kind of magic, is it?"

"Oh no," Meg said. "It's just that dragons are very clever, and I suppose that's how they talk. Naturally."

"Hmmph," Janna said. "What's his name?"

"His name?" Meg asked, stalling. "His name is, um—"

"Ladybug," Cam suggested. "After all that red."

Meg grimaced. "No."

"It'll have to be *Laddy*bug, seeing as how you call him a he," Janna said.

"I'm not sure," Meg said, surprised. "It's just a feeling I have."

"Laddy, then," Janna said. She reached out a tentative hand to scratch the dragon between the ears.

"It's not dignified!" Meg exclaimed.

"Names choose themselves," Janna said easily.

Meg gave up. For all the splendor of his coloring, the dragon did have a puppyish look. *I'll give you a grand name when you grow up,* she promised him privately.

The dragon blinked up at her.

"What does he eat?" Janna asked.

Meg remembered something. "Cam! The treasure."

Cam pulled gold and jewels out of his pockets, piling them on the kitchen table.

"Oh, my," said Cam's sister.

"I've got more," Meg said. "To prove something to my father." She gestured at the shining mass. "But this will make the dragon feel more at home. And you can use part of it to pay for his food."

Janna nodded, momentarily speechless. She seemed

to have forgotten her hand, which was still stroking the dragon's head.

"He eats rabbits," said Cam, finally answering Janna's question. "And bats."

"He likes his nose rubbed," Meg added. "What else? Sometimes he sets things on fire."

Janna jerked her hand back. "What!"

"*For* you!" Cam said hastily. "He'll light the fire in the morning, is what she means."

"He'll even glow if you ask him to. For a night-light," Meg put in.

Janna raised a sardonic brow. "I see."

Not taking any chances, Meg woke the dragon up to say goodbye. *I'll be back in a few days. Don't burn anything except what the nice lady tells you to,* she thought at him firmly.

The dragon regarded her with sleepy eyes.

And for heaven's sake, don't eat the cats!

Morning at the castle found Queen Istilda fiddling with her embroidery, her mind cloudy with worry as her ladies-in-waiting gabbled.

"So Lady Calissa said, 'I could never love a black-haired man!' " one named Maude explained. "And Sir Howard went right off to the other side of the ballroom!"

"A tear ran down his cheek," Eugenia intoned.

"Did you see it?" asked Florence.

"No, but Lord Faradel's squire did."

Whereupon the queen poked herself with her needle. Her ladies stared.

"Your Majesty, are you all right?" Florence whispered.

"Hmm?" said the queen.

"You haven't pricked your finger since—"

"Since *ever*," said Eugenia breathlessly.

The queen peered at her embroidery. "Why, so I have," she murmured. Her gaze lifted to the wall and lingered. There was a stunned silence, after which Her Majesty said, "I'd like to be alone."

Three bewildered ladies crept out of the room, closing the door softly behind them.

The queen sat a moment longer before she threw down her embroidery and went to the window. Across the meadow, the tower squatted like a troll in the friendly morning light. One of the older guards paced before it. "How are you keeping, daughter?" the queen said. A tear rather more real than Sir Howard's slid down her cheek.

The morning was still for a few moments. Then Queen Istilda saw someone hurrying across the grass toward the tower, carrying a basket. Meg's maid—Dilly, wasn't it? The girl reached the tower and spoke to the guard. Argued even, by the look of it. Finally the man marched back toward the castle. As he neared the wall, Queen Istilda could see his disgruntled face.

The queen frowned. Surely the *girl* hadn't been sent to guard Margaret! She watched Dilly, who seemed to be calling up to the window. No face appeared there, but two servants emerged from behind the tower. The princess's maid began to talk with the newcomers, the gardener's boy and a girl with light brown braids.

All three looked up at the window now, and at last someone came to look out. The queen felt a pang at the sight of that thin, white face—poor child.

Suddenly the prisoner climbed into view, perching on the sill: not her daughter at all, but a skinny boy!

Queen Istilda gasped. Where was Margaret? She watched the girl with the braids again. The queen lifted her brows.

The skinny boy had produced a stout rope and was scrambling down the tower wall. When he reached the bottom, the four young people began talking. They even ate some of the food from Dilly's basket. Finally Dilly walked back toward the castle. The gardener's boy and— the queen was quite sure now—Margaret went around the tower, disappearing from sight. They left the other boy behind. He picked up a spear and stood at attention, guarding the empty prison.

Queen Istilda jumped up and went to the chamber door, even putting out her hand to open it. Instead she stopped herself and returned to the window, a small smile on her lips.

It took Vantor a great deal of talk to convince the twin princes to go on without him, now that they were playing at rescuer.

"You could ride to the castle on our cow," Dagle suggested.

"We'll share a hearty breakfast, gather provisions, and set out again," Dorn added.

Vantor seemed to be holding himself in check. "I'll be along later. I'm going to try to find some evidence of the scoundrels who did this," Vantor told them.

"We'll help!" said Dorn.

"No," Vantor said regretfully, "we can't keep you from your own purposes any longer."

"If you're sure," an earnest Dagle said.

"Very."

With hearty farewells, the twins set off down the hill toward the castle.

"Wait!" Vantor called. They looked back. He ran toward them awkwardly, still stiff from being tied up. Vantor lowered his voice. "Best keep this between ourselves. We'll get further finding these ruffians if we can spy about like gentlemen."

"Of course!" The princes smiled, and Vantor watched them go.

Dagle and Dorn walked awhile in silence. Then Dorn said, "He didn't want anyone to know those bandits caught him, eh?"

"Nope," said Dagle.

"Felt a great fool, didn't he?"

"Yep," said Dagle.

"Moo," said the cow.

Grubby and bleary-eyed, Meg and Cam shared their breakfast with Dilly out of Meg's morning basket. Nort had already eaten the last of the food in Meg's tower. "Good thing I was up there," he said proudly.

"Good thing," Meg agreed. She and Cam had left Janna's after midnight, crossing a broad stretch of farmland and the Witch's Wood, too. When they reached the tower, exhausted, Meg and Cam piled up leaves a short distance inside the woods and slept till morning, waiting for Nort to come on guard.

"We saw Arbel there still and didn't know what had happened," Meg said.

"*We* didn't know what had happened," Dilly exclaimed.

So Meg told Dilly and Nort all about the dragon and Vantor and the cave, and Cam told them about the night journey and the twin princes and his sister's farm.

Then it was Dilly's turn to explain what had happened over at the witch's cottage. Meg wasn't very sympathetic about the frog princes. "They'd be fine if they had just left her alone." When she heard about Bain's plan, she was more concerned. "Magic?"

" 'Fight fire with fire,' he said."

"Where would he get magic?" Cam wondered.

"In town, of course," Nort said. "There are lots of wizards in Crown."

Meg nodded. "My mother called a wizard once, when she'd lost her ruby necklace."

"I heard all the wizards were fakes," said Cam.

"Some are. But a few are quite good," Nort said.

"So that's where Bain will have gone," Meg concluded. "We'd better go warn the witch."

"I have to get back," said Dilly, disappointed. "Sterga yelled at me for half an hour last night."

"I suppose I'm standing guard again," Nort said with a sigh.

"If you don't mind," Meg said hopefully.

Nort picked up his spear as Dilly took her leave. Meg and Cam set off in the opposite direction, deeper into the woods.

When Vantor reached the cave, he nearly tripped over a snoring Horace. The prince kicked his manservant. "Untie him!" he snapped at the others, stalking into the cave.

Vantor emerged to find a guardsman giving Horace a drink of water.

"It's all gone!" Vantor raged. "All my treasure is gone!" He kicked Horace again. "What happened?!"

Horace grasped his sore leg protectively. "First, a couple of them stole the dragon and attacked me inside the cave."

"Who did?" said Vantor, his hand reaching for his sword. It wasn't there.

"Where's your sword?" Horace asked.

The rest of the men took a step back as Vantor's face darkened. "We were ambushed by bandits."

"Many, many bandits," one of the men clarified.

Horace winced, standing up. "The ones who got at *me*—well, the first lot—seemed very young."

"You were attacked by children?" Vantor said derisively. He paused. "What do you mean, the first lot?"

Horace saw the expressions on the faces around him and reconsidered. "Must have been bandits. And the dragon burned me."

Someone chuckled.

"That little creature?" Vantor asked.

"Fire's fire," Horace said, sullen now.

"Go on."

"When I chased them, another man attacked me from behind."

"And then? What did you hear?"

Horace looked vague. "Footsteps?"

"Fell asleep, didn't 'e?" one of the men jeered.

Vantor clenched his fists and his jaw. Next he said a great many words so noxious even Horace didn't know them. Finally, he stopped long enough to announce, "We're going after the bandits. After our gold!"

The men gave a ragged cheer. Vantor pointed at one of them. "You. Go into town and buy me another horse."

"Are we going to set up our secret camp now?" a great bear of a man asked.

"We will set up our secret camp," Vantor explained sarcastically, "when we get our secret gold back to put in it!"

"Yes, sir," the man said, oblivious to the prince's tone.

For his part, Horace found a rock and sat down again. "I've a different task for you," Vantor told him. "Get that witch."

Horace whitened. "She'll turn me into a frog."

"Attack her from behind. You know all about that," Vantor said.

"Yes, Your Highness."

"Now," Vantor told him.

Horace rose and started down the hill, limping slightly.

"Watch out for children and baby dragons!" he heard, followed by the sound of Vantor's men laughing.

Gorba's clearing was quiet, with no sign of any princes. Meg walked right up to the cottage and knocked.

The witch opened the door. "Oh, it's you."

"You're in grave danger," Meg blurted.

"Do you have amnesia?" the witch asked. "You told me that already."

"It's a new danger," Cam said, stepping forward.

The witch scratched her bulgy nose. "Who are you?"

"I'm the gardener's boy up at the castle," Cam explained.

The witch looked from Meg to Cam and back to Meg. "I see," she said slyly. "Then *she* must be a princess in disguise."

Meg's jaw dropped. "How did you know?" she squeaked.

"Stands to reason." The witch sighed and beamed. "True love. And such young love."

"What?" said Cam.

"She thinks we're in love," Meg told him.

Cam made a face.

"I'm Gorba," the witch chirped. "Come in, come in! Mind the frogs."

Cam and Meg trailed her into the cottage, stepping over half a dozen frogs. Gorba shooed several more off the sofa. "Sit down. Would you like a cup of tea?"

Bewildered, Cam and Meg sat. They watched the frogs as the witch bustled about making tea. Finally, she plopped herself down on the flowered armchair and served it. Meg noticed the teacups were shaped like skulls, with green worms twisting out the eyeholes for handles. "They were my grandmother's," Gorba said.

"They match the curtains," Meg said approvingly.

"Now." Gorba cleared a protesting bullfrog off the table and leaned forward. "How can I help the course of your love to run smooth?"

10

—um," Meg said.

Gorba smiled, revealing gaps in her long yellow teeth. "No need to be coy. Here you are. The princess and the gardener's boy."

"Cam," he muttered.

"You're running away, aren't you?" the witch asked.

"Sort of," Meg said.

"You see," Cam tried, "a prince is bringing a spell to attack you with."

"Very sweet," Gorba said, "but you're changing the subject. Do you want me to turn a rival suitor into a frog?"

Meg looked intrigued. "Vantor," she whispered behind her hand, but Cam shook his head.

"We know you're not worried about princes," Meg explained, "but one of them is going to pay a wizard to make some magic to harm you."

Gorba chortled. "Those old goats? I can handle anything they throw at me!"

Someone knocked heavily on the door.

The witch got up. "Don't!" Meg cried. It was too late. Gorba was already opening the door. But she bent down to scoot one of her frogs aside, and a flash of light flew right over her head into the room.

Cam and Meg tried to dive out of the way. Instead they bumped heads and the spell reached them, striking Cam full in the chest. Meg scrambled up, only to see Cam struggle, floating in midair, then shrink, shrink, shrink as Prince Bain burst in the door, tipping the witch over.

He was halfway across the cottage, and all that was left of Cam was a little triangular box made of silver. The thing still glowed slightly. Meg reached for it, but Bain was faster. He scooped it up and leaped into the corner, a dagger in one hand and the spell in the other.

"Give him to me!" Meg cried.

Bain only grinned.

Gorba glared at the prince. "You'll have to find your own pond when I'm through with you," she sputtered.

"Surrender, witch," Bain said, unconcerned.

Meg stepped forward, her eyes on the little box.

Recognition dawned on Bain's face. "You're the girl who stole the dragon," he said, surprised.

How did he know? Meg wondered.

"You did?" Gorba asked Meg.

Bain tossed the silver box in the air and caught it. "I'll trade you this boy for the beast," he said.

Before Meg could answer, the witch said, "*I'll give*

you safe passage out of my house in exchange for the boy." She began inching toward the intruder.

"I suppose it's safe to say I've lost the element of surprise," Bain remarked, eyeing the frogs. He looked at Meg again. "Who are you working for?"

"Myself."

Bain smiled sweetly. "Then we have something in common. Now, take me to the dragon, and I'll give your friend back."

Meg took a step closer. "How do I know you'll keep your word?"

Gorba was nearly within arm's reach of him now.

Bain tucked the box in his pocket. "A valuable lad, even if he isn't a witch." With that he plunged through the half-open window, bursting the shutters wide.

"Cam!" Meg shouted. She ran to the window, throwing herself out after Bain. Meg hit the ground hard and scrambled to her feet to chase the prince, but she could not see him. A twig snapped. Meg rushed at the sound, but nothing was there. Bain had disappeared into the forest, and Cam had disappeared with him.

"Come inside, child," Gorba said at the window.

Meg ranged among the trees for a long time before she admitted she wasn't going to find the prince or his prisoner. Finally she made herself go back to the witch's cottage. Her shoulder ached where she had landed on it.

"Sit down," Gorba said.

Meg sank onto the sofa, still unable to believe what had happened.

"That thing was meant for me, was it?" Gorba asked thoughtfully.

"It was." Meg glanced up, suddenly hopeful. "Can you change him back? When I find him?"

Gorba didn't meet Meg's eyes. "Magic like that needs a counterspell."

"And you can't—"

"From the wizard who made it," Gorba added.

"I'll have to find the wizard," Meg said.

"That you will."

The two sat in silence for a bit. At last Meg said, "It's not safe for you here."

"I've got my frog spell, haven't I?"

"If one prince thought of that magic, so will another," Meg told Gorba. She ought to finish what she had started. And besides, she thought dolefully, she should tell Janna about Cam. "I know a place you can hide out for a while."

"Hide out?" the witch growled. "I've got my pride!"

"It will be like a vacation."

"And the boys?"

Meg looked around for boys. "You mean the frogs?"

The witch nodded.

"Haven't they been prisoners long enough?"

Gorba began to laugh, and every frog in the room croaked along. The witch wiped her eyes and spoke. "I've tried sending them home time and time again."

"What?"

"They like it here," the witch said simply. She imitated a manly royal voice. "Oh, Gorba, me and Prince Kelorian were just going to square off for the weekly leaping finals. Please leave us be."

Meg gaped.

"It's true," the witch said. "I've only had one go back in I don't know how many years. And he was allergic to flies."

"Well . . ." Meg watched the frogs for a moment. In the nearest tub, a leopard frog swam laps with obvious enjoyment. The bullfrog rumbled contentedly.

Someone else knocked heavily on the door. "You see?" Meg hissed.

This time the witch stood well to one side of the door to swing it open. The porch seemed empty. Gorba shrugged. She was about to close the door when a man burst around the jamb and threw a cloak over her head. "I've got you now!" he shouted, but a faint muttering could be heard beneath the cloak, and the man shriveled away to the floor.

The witch pulled the cloak off. She and Meg looked down, bemused. "Have you ever done a salamander before?" Meg asked.

"No." Gorba picked the little orange-and-black creature up and slipped it onto the edge of the bathtub, where it eyed the frogs fearfully. "Can't think what happened."

"That was Prince Vantor's man," Meg observed.

"Not a prince." The witch frowned. "Maybe he was a duke or an earl."

"Maybe," Meg agreed, a little confused.

The witch folded her arms. "I suppose you'll need help getting your true love back."

"Cam," Meg said, resigned.

"It's gotten very annoying, all these hoodlums mucking through my wood."

Meg waited.

"I'd better come along," Gorba told her.

"And the boys?"

"And the boys."

"We haven't got time," Prince Dorn told his brother, pushing a branch out of the way.

"It won't take long."

"If they catch us, we're right out of this."

Dagle gave him a look. "We're not afraid of dragons or witches. Are we afraid of a scrawny prime minister?"

"The witch wasn't home," Dorn remarked.

Dagle stopped. "Are you afraid of *princesses*?"

Dorn waved his hand. "That satin. Those batting eyelashes. The eerie swishing of fans. It's not—"

"Not as sure as a sword blade?" Dagle asked kindly. "Don't worry, I've got just the weapon for all that."

The two princes came to the edge of the woods behind the princess's tower.

"What weapon?" Dorn asked.

"Poetry."

Dorn stared at his brother. "That's what you were doing yesterday. Making up a poem."

"And I finished it," Dagle said.

The twin princes of Hanaby Keep came around the tower, startling a skinny young guard.

"Hey there," the boy said indignantly. "Be off with you!"

Two hands held out gold coins. The guard's expression changed. "In five minutes, that is," he said. "Don't tell the others." He turned his eyes nervously up to the tower.

The princes followed his gaze with their own. "Is she enjoying her sojourn?" Dagle asked.

"Enjoying?" The boy practically choked. "She's taken a vow of silence," he managed to say at last.

"Will she come to the window?" Dorn said.

The guardsboy shook his head vigorously. "She's rather occupied. All that sojourning, you know."

Dagle cleared his throat. "O Princess!" he called. "My brother and I have come to court you—"

"At great personal peril, tell her," Dorn whispered.

"At great personal peril," Dagle repeated. "I will now read a poem to you, written by myself, about your legendary beauty and—ahem—so forth." Dagle fished a battered piece of parchment from the pouch that hung at his hip and read in a strong, pleasant voice:

"*O glorimous, glimmerous lady,*
O Princess most worthy and fond,
Your hair is as shining as armor,
Your eyes they do shimmer like ponds."

"Ponds?" Dorn repeated.

"Shh," said Dagle. The guardsboy made an odd noise. Dagle went on, slamming his free hand over his heart.

> *"Our twin hearts, they beat in your service*
> *As we conquer the dragonly beast,*
> *Then as soon as we've finished the others,*
> *We'll bring you right down for the feast."*

"What others?" Dorn hissed.

"Princess, when I say 'others' I am referring to the witch and the bandits," Dagle said loudly. "And now I conclude."

"Good," said the guard, then pretended he hadn't.

Dagle frowned at him.

> *"The true love for which you've been waiting*
> *E'er since the glad day you were born,*
> *Is standing right under your window*
> *In the form of good Dagle or Dorn."*

Dorn smiled. "That ended nicely."

"I'm sure she's touched," the guard said. He looked over at the castle. "But you'd better go."

"Well now." Dagle seemed uncertain for the first time.

Dorn brightened. "Farewell, Princess!" he called.

"Farewell!" Dagle echoed. In a softer voice he told his brother, "Let's go fetch our cow."

Bidding the young guard goodbye, they went back around the tower.

"Do you think she liked it?" Dagle asked.

"Of course," Dorn said staunchly. "Love is sprouting in her heart right now, like a violet in springtime."

"Why, Dorn, you're a poet, too!"

Dorn blushed.

"I'm not in love!" said the princess of Greeve for the fifteenth time. "And your spell's failed again."

The witch turned around. Behind her, frogs were plopping out of the air onto the forest floor like fat raindrops. They lay half-stunned, gazing up at Gorba reproachfully. A single salamander curled in their midst like an orange-and-black question mark. "It isn't my spell," the witch told Meg for the fifth time. "It was my grandmother's, and her work was unreliable."

Gorba removed the spell, a dark blue scarf with too many eyes, from around her neck and whapped it against the nearest tree branch. The scarf giggled. Gorba ground her teeth. "Floating. Frogs."

"And salamander," Meg put in.

"*Obviously.*"

The scarf's eyes flickered like stars in a night sky. The frogs rose jerkily back into the air, until they were level with the top of Meg's head. "Three feet, since you

keep dropping them," the witch said acidly. The frogs
swooped partway to the ground and hovered, ribbeting
in a nervous chorus. The salamander loop-the-looped
once and joined his green companions.

Gorba flipped the scarf around her neck as she
stalked off between the trees. The frogs followed her like
the wobbling green train of a very odd court gown.

"I still don't see why you couldn't float these bottles
and bags, too," Meg said. She was carrying a heavy pack
filled with what Gorba would call only "supplies."

"Can't risk any of that dropping."

Meg adjusted the straps and soldiered on. Really, it
was a beautiful day. If she hadn't been so worried about
Cam, she would have enjoyed the sunlight through the
leaves, the flash of birds' wings, the red brush of a fox
flickering through the undergrowth . . . The fox had
been trailing them for some time now, Meg realized.
"That fox wants frog for lunch," she observed.

Gorba turned around and locked eyes with the fox.
She said something in yips and barks that sent him scrambling away through the forest without a backward glance.

Meg was thrilled. "Will you teach me to speak fox?"
she asked the witch.

But Gorba insisted on turning the topic to romance.
"First tell me how you feel when you gaze deep into the
gardener's boy's eyes."

Meg put her hands on her hips. "He's my friend.
That's *all*!" she exclaimed.

The witch seemed to hear her this time. "Friend, is

it?" Gorba was silent for so long that the frogs started dropping again and had to be put back by the scarf. Meg noticed the surprise of several flies when the green menaces followed them into the air.

Meg was just beginning to believe Gorba had accepted her word about her friendship with Cam when the witch asked, too casually, "Do you happen to have half a ring on a chain about your neck?"

Meg groaned. "No!" She rushed to climb over a fallen tree, trying to get out of earshot of the persistent old woman. Instead she scraped her shin and the witch caught up with her, frogs and all.

"Your young 'friend' will have the other half, of course," Gorba said. "He's just biding his time."

"He's not—"

"Then he'll drop it in your goblet at your wedding dinner, and just as you're about to marry the wrong prince, you'll remember everything."

"I told you, I don't *have* half a ring!" Meg cried.

"Maybe," Gorba said, her eyes bright, "you've forgotten that, too."

The witch's scarf snickered. Meg scowled at it when Gorba wasn't looking. Then she shook her head. Who cared what the witch thought? The only thing that mattered was rescuing Cam. "Whatever he is," Meg said, "I want him back."

"That's right, dear," Gorba said smugly. She whistled a well-known Greevian love ballad the rest of the way through the forest, with the frogs providing a backbeat.

II

T WASN'T HARD TO FIND JANNA'S FARM IN the daylight. The only trouble was keeping other people from seeing the witch and her frogs along the way. Whenever Meg saw someone coming, she would shoo Gorba off the road. Once, when they came around a bend and saw a peddler nearly upon them, the witch said a sharp word to her scarf. All of the frogs shot up into the branches of the nearest tree, where they pretended to be leaves.

The peddler's face paled. "Did you see something just now? A sort of green cloud?"

Meg tried to look baffled.

"The gnats are bad," Gorba said conversationally.

She and Meg bought some needles and thread from the man to distract him from dangerous topics. He seemed inclined to chat, but they managed to send him on his way, and Gorba retrieved her frogs.

When the little group finally reached Hookhorn

Farm, Meg asked Gorba to wait out of sight while she spoke to Cam's sister.

Meg found Janna chasing the dragon around the chicken yard with a broom. Laddy was gulping a string of sausages as fast as he could. He swallowed the last with a snap and flopped down, rolling over onto his back.

"You want me to scratch your belly after you stole my lunch?" Janna demanded.

"He seems well," Meg said, unshouldering her heavy pack.

"If it isn't the royal pain," Janna said wryly. "Come for your baby?"

"No," Meg said. But she knelt and called to the creature. The dragon trotted to her side, laying his head against her knee. "Well, hello there. Who's my beautiful boy?" she asked, scratching him between the ears. For a moment she forgot why she had come.

"Where's Cam?" Janna asked, reminding her abruptly.

Meg opened her mouth, but Gorba spoke first, stepping around the corner of the farmhouse. "It isn't much of a resort."

"Resort?" Janna said. "Who is this, Meg?"

"It's more of a refuge, a sanctuary," Meg told the witch.

"Oh, really?" Janna asked, her mouth tightening. "What are you up to now?"

"This poor old woman—"

"Witch," Gorba corrected.

"Poor old *witch* Gorba has been hounded from her home—"

"Princed, more like," Gorba said.

"And needs a place to stay. Just for a little while," Meg finished hastily, before Gorba could interrupt again.

Janna folded her arms. "This is *not* an inn, young lady. You can take your dragon and your witch—begging your pardon, ma'am—and find a proper place to put them!"

"She said she'd help us get Cam back," Meg said quietly. "He's gone."

Janna looked from the somber old face to the somber young one. Her own face fell. "Come inside," she told them.

Nearby, a bullfrog croaked.

Janna turned around. Dozens of golden eyes were peering out from beneath the lowest rung of the fence.

"I brought a few friends," Gorba said.

After Janna had heard Meg's story, she agreed to let Gorba stay. There was no more talk of Laddy's leaving. Meg suspected Janna was growing attached to the little dragon. He hadn't eaten the cats; in fact, the cats now napped around him as if he were a spare hearth.

But Janna refused to let the frogs in the house. "Frogs in the frog pond," she said, and Gorba was forced to send her companions out to the end of the pasture.

"They'll mix with common frogs," Gorba muttered, but Janna's mind was made up.

Over a cup of tea, Meg and Gorba and Janna sat at the kitchen table discussing how to rescue Cam. Even though the witch was nervous about leaving the frogs on the farm, she offered to come with Meg to find the wizard. "What would you say to him?" Meg asked, afraid she already knew the answer.

"I know how to address wizards," Gorba said loftily. She grimaced, frightening the cats. "Cut-rate wannabe witches."

"There's something else that would help me more," Meg said. She had been thinking during the long whistling walk through the forest. "I need a way to stay out of the tower."

"But you are out."

"She wants to keep it that way," Janna remarked, sitting down in the rocker and putting her feet up on Laddy's warm back.

The three of them considered the possibilities. "What about a spell to make Arbel forget he's seen me?" Meg asked.

"He'd forget his own name, his wife and children, everything," Gorba said. So that wouldn't do.

"You could take the floating frog spell," Gorba said. She tossed her scarf onto the table, where it stared at Janna till she blinked.

"The tower is very high," Meg said pointedly.

"Use it to fly the rope up and down," the witch suggested.

"Can it tie a knot?"

"Why don't you try hiding the rope?" Janna asked. "Paint it a special color or something."

Meg sat up. "Make it invisible!"

Gorba brightened. "That I can do."

Within moments, the witch had taken over Janna's kitchen and was telling Meg to open the pack the princess had carried through the forest. "It's all labeled," Gorba said, grabbing a small saucepan. "I'll need cockroach toes, mouse's blink, and pickled fog, to begin with."

Janna opened her mouth, then closed it and opened a book instead, apparently determined not to let these proceedings ruffle her.

Meg rummaged through the pack.

"Careful!" Gorba snapped. She poured a little water from the teakettle into the saucepan.

Meg pulled out the first bottle and handed it to the witch.

When Meg had found everything, Gorba surveyed the row of ingredients critically. "We're missing frog's tears and the farthest tail-hair of a cat."

Janna looked up from her book. "You leave my cats alone."

Gorba ignored her. "Get the cat's hair, Princess." Gorba took Howie out of her pocket to tell him a terribly sad story about a frog whose tongue got tangled up in a fishing line.

"Sorry," Meg said to Janna, and began stalking the cats.

In the end, Meg left with a packet of sweet rolls from Janna and an invisibility spell from Gorba. She had only had three more arguments with the witch before Gorba finally agreed to stay behind. Now Gorba was fussing about the spell again.

"One drop should do it," she advised. "It's quite strong. Maybe even half a drop. Or two-thirds of a drop."

"All right," Meg said, wondering how anyone could pour two-thirds of a drop.

The witch followed Meg out to the gate, with Janna and the dragon close behind. "How are you going to pay the wizard?" Janna asked suddenly.

Meg patted her pocket. "Dragon gold. Remember?"

"Is that why the creature is sniffing your ankle?" Gorba asked.

Meg reached down to Laddy. "Goodbye, silly."

When she stood up again, Gorba shoved the blue scarf at her. "Take it," she said. "I've given it strict orders to obey you."

Meg looked dubious.

"It'll be better than nothing in a pinch," the witch argued.

Meg tucked the scarf into her pocket, pulling her hand out fast at the feel of tiny eyelashes brushing her fingers. "Thank you," she told Gorba. She hugged the old woman impulsively.

Then she hugged Janna. "I'll bring him home," she promised.

"Please," Janna said.

Meg set off down the road. She had only taken a dozen paces when she turned back. "You know, half a ring would fall right off the chain," she called.

Gorba and Janna waved as Meg went on her way.

"Young love," Gorba murmured affectionately.

It was nearly sunset when Meg reached the tower.

"Hurry," Nort said.

"I'm not going up there," said Meg.

"Well, neither am I!"

"All right. Watch this," Meg said mysteriously, taking a tiny vial from her pocket. She tipped a drop of dark liquid onto the end of the rope. The drop sparked and began running upward. As it went, the rope disappeared from sight. And then—the entire tower disappeared.

Meg and Nort goggled. Meg grabbed Nort's hand abruptly, pulling him after her. "We've got to hide!" They rushed into the woods.

"I'm not supposed to leave my post!" Nort argued, tugging free and moving toward the tower, wild-eyed.

Meg jumped in front of him. "Your post has left *you*," she said. "Do you want to tell Hanak what happened?"

Nort's shoulders sagged. "They'll blame me. I'll be sent home—or thrown in the dungeons."

Meg was still trying to comfort him when Dilly crashed through the bushes, calling Nort's name.

"Here we are," Meg said.

Dilly made her way through the trees to stand in front of them, panting like a bellows. The instant she caught her breath, she cried, "What have you done? Hanak was just going to tell the king when I left!"

As if to confirm her words, people began pouring across the meadow from the castle toward the space where Meg's prison should have been. One of Hanak's men ran ahead of the others and right into the invisible tower, falling hard to the ground. Meg and Nort laughed nervously.

"It's not funny!" Dilly hissed.

"He'll be all right," Meg told her. The guard staggered to his feet. "See?"

"They're going to see *you* in another minute," Dilly said.

The three friends hid themselves more carefully where they could watch the goings-on in the meadow. King Stromgard stormed over to the tower and touched it. Then he started shouting at everyone. Hanak felt about the tower wall. He must have discovered the rope: he called one of the pages over, pointing upward.

The page took hold of the invisible rope and climbed into the sky. It was a wonderful sight, especially when the page disappeared through Meg's invisible window. After a few minutes, his head popped out into the air and said something to the waiting crowd.

"I'm not there," Meg explained.

Dilly snorted.

The page came slowly down as the king gave more orders. Finally, the king turned to go back to the castle. The queen stood staring at the woods for a moment before she followed him.

"Almost as if she sees us," Nort whispered.

Hanak stayed behind long enough to post a guard on the unseen tower. The other castle folk who had come out to see what the excitement was about must have decided nothing else was going to happen. They trickled away toward the castle.

"Definitely the dungeons," Nort said woefully.

"They'll think you were attacked when Meg was," Dilly observed.

"Attacked by who?" he asked.

"The witch," Meg said, standing up and brushing the leaves from her skirt. "That's who they'll blame."

"Aren't you going to tell me what happened?" Dilly asked.

"And me!" said Nort.

"I've lost Cam," Meg told them.

"In the woods?" Dilly said.

"In Prince Bain's pocket."

Meg ignored the clamor of questions that followed this pronouncement, leading her friends farther into the woods. Soon the princess found a small clearing. "Sit, please," she said. Nort and Dilly plopped down on a fallen tree.

Meg perched on a stump and told them everything that had happened. "We've got to get Cam back. And we've got to find the wizard who made the spell," she concluded.

"I saw Prince Bain at the castle just before the alarm was raised," Dilly said.

"Cam's in a silver box?" Nort said. "How big is it?"

"It would fit in my hand."

"Everyone will be after the witch now," Dilly pointed out.

"They won't find her unless they speak fox," said Meg. "We met a peddler—but I don't think he'll realize it was us he saw."

"Maybe Prince Bain left the box in his room," Dilly said. "I could take some linens up and search for it."

"Maybe." Meg looked at Dilly's hopeful face. "It's worth a try."

"I could challenge him to noble combat," Nort offered.

"You're coming with me into Crown to find that wizard."

"Wizard?" Nort swallowed.

"You said you wanted an adventure," Dilly reminded him.

Nort squared his skinny shoulders. "Right. We're off to see the wizard."

"They'll be looking for you, too," Dilly told Meg.

"They'll be looking for a princess. I'm not a princess at the moment."

"How will I find you again?" Dilly asked.

"Meet us in the morning—" Meg stopped to think. "Not here. There will be princes in the woods. It'll have to be by the frog pond."

"What about those bandits?" Nort said. "Aren't we going to capture them anymore?"

"Cam comes first," Meg said sternly.

"Besides," Dilly told Nort, "Meg's already completed two of the three tasks. She's practically won the contest."

"She hasn't actually *destroyed* anything," Nort began, but he trailed off at the sight of Meg's expression.

The torchlit royal courtyard was in a state of uproar. Fewer than a dozen princes were left, but they seemed to make as much noise as the original number, arguing about how to rescue the princess from the witch.

"I'll have my hounds after the evil crone," said a watery-eyed prince with an eastern accent.

"And if she flew away on her broom?" Vantor inquired sardonically.

"Perhaps it was the bandits," Prince Bain interjected.

Vantor frowned at him. "Bandits? This has witch written all over it!"

"Unless the witch is working hand in hand with the bandits."

Vantor pointedly turned his back on Bain.

Inside the castle, the king was saying to his queen, "Our daughter's been abducted. Are you going to speak to me now?"

"I told you not to put her up there," Queen Istilda retorted. Then she turned and swept away down the corridor.

The king glared at the prime minister. "These are *not* the kind of results I meant," he rumbled.

Anyone watching the queen might have noticed that her pace was a bit less sedate than usual as she returned to her quarters. "Find my daughter's maid," she told Maude. Her lady-in-waiting scurried away.

Unaware of the hullabaloo at the castle, Dorn and Dagle stepped back to admire their handiwork.

"It's a beautiful hole," said Dagle.

"Pit, you mean. A trap is much more than a mere hole."

"You're right, brother." Dagle squatted to peer into the gaping mouth of the pit. "Do you think it's large enough to hold a dragon?"

"Wings fully spread, or furled?"

"They'll have to be furled."

"Let's make it just a little wider," his twin told him.

The two princes wielded their shovels with renewed

determination. Dirt flew out of the hole like upside-down, discolored rain.

Over by the wind-twisted pines, the cow chewed on a pile of straw, dreaming of lost green pastures as the sun slowly set.

12

ILLY BUSTLED ALONG A PASSAGEWAY WITH her arms full of towels. When she reached Prince Bain's room, she rapped smartly on the door. She wasn't surprised when no one answered: Prince Bain was in the courtyard with everyone else. Dilly pushed the door open and slipped into the empty room, closing the door behind her.

Some of the princes left clutter about, cloaks thrown over chairs, scabbards on the beds. Not Prince Bain. The only sign of his presence was a single silk shirt hung neatly inside his wardrobe. Dilly's heart sank. "Cam isn't here," she said to the silence.

Still, she searched the room, lifting the pillows and the mattress, peering inside the wooden chest at the foot of the bed. Nowhere could she find the little box Meg had described.

When she finished, Dilly tidied up and left with her towels. She was nearly to the stairs when someone called her name, and she glanced back to see Maude, one of the queen's ladies, coming toward her.

Maude hurried her away to the queen's chambers. Dilly's heart pounded, though she tried to calm it. Meg's mother wants to know if I have any ideas about what happened, she told herself. That's all.

The lady-in-waiting followed Dilly inside. Dilly had been within the queen's chambers only once before, when the queen was at a state dinner and a senior maid had wanted to impress Dilly with the beauty of the place. The queen's chambers were hung with hundreds of fluting lengths of pink and gold glass that chimed delicately when a breeze was allowed to drift through the windows and shimmered when the light struck them. That day Dilly had liked coming into the queen's own rooms, but not now—especially after the queen dismissed all three of her ladies. They looked appalled to be sent out.

The door clicked shut. "Sit down," the queen said, indicating a little chair with one graceful hand. Dilly bobbed a curtsy and took her seat.

"Dilly," the queen said firmly, "where is my daughter?"

Dilly's mouth opened, but nothing came out. She snapped it shut.

"Young lady, I saw you with Margaret and her friends at the foot of the tower this very morning."

Dilly froze, panic-stricken. Nort was right! And she was going to be the first one thrown into the dungeons.

The queen's expression softened. "I'm not going to punish you," she said. "But I want to know: is my daughter safe?"

Dilly nodded cautiously.

"Has she been abducted?"

Dilly shook her head.

The queen allowed herself a smile. "Tell me, then: is Margaret responsible for the current state of the tower?"

Dilly's own lips quirked as she nodded.

The queen grew serious again. "I trust that you will put my child's safety first, even before your loyalty to her wishes."

Dilly thought this over. She nodded once more.

"It's been lovely talking with you," the queen said dryly. "You may go now."

Dilly escaped past the queen's curious ladies into the halls of the castle, hoping with all her heart that Meg was truly safe as she prowled the city, trying to find a wizard. The fact that Nort was with her seemed small comfort.

Meg had been in Crown at night before, if riding along the main boulevard in a lantern-lit carriage surrounded by armed guards counted. Her mother had also taken her to the marketplace by day, but Hanak's men had made sure Meg never came close to any grubby sort of contact with the city folk. The castle grounds had been her world.

Of course, since then she'd shared tea with a witch, escaped a dragon's cave, and entered an actual farmhouse, Meg thought. Fine preparation for this night's adventures. Unfortunately, she was having to rely on Nort for directions, and he was as nervous and high-strung as one of Vantor's horses.

"Where do the wizards live?" Meg asked patiently.

"It's not like that," Nort told her. "They're secretive."

Whereupon Meg tried offering a gold coin to a passing beggar to get directions. The beggar mumbled incomprehensibly, but within moments of that encounter, a small group of boys began following Meg and Nort from street to darkened street. "I can take one of them, but that's all," Nort whispered.

Meg stopped abruptly. The nearest boy bumped into her and fell down. "Watch where you're going!" he snarled. The other boys closed in.

They reminded Meg of that pack of princes, except for the raggedy clothes. "Which one of you's the leader?" she demanded.

The boys hesitated, then the biggest one thumbed his chest. "I'm Dock. What's it to you?"

"I'm looking for a wizard."

"And who might you be?" Dock said.

Meg improvised. "I'm a witch. The wizard is my uncle."

"Where're your warts?" one boy jeered.

Meg stood her ground. "Help me or clear off."

"She's telling us to clear off," someone called. "You hear that, Dock?"

The tall boy stared at Meg. "What kind of help?"

"Gonna cost you," said another one. He spat on the cobblestones.

"You're no witch," Dock said.

"Apprentice witch," Nort suggested.

"Do some magic!" yelled a skinny blond boy.

The circle of faces was eager and hostile in the dimly lit street. "I can make something invisible," she told them.

Dock picked up a rock and held it out.

"If I do, will you help me?" Meg asked.

"First the magic."

Nort touched Meg's arm. "Don't make any deals!"

Meg ignored him. She took out Gorba's vial and poured a minuscule drop onto the rock. It flashed and disappeared.

The boys' eyes widened. Dock hefted the invisible rock with a slow smile. Then he passed it around to the others. When it was back in his hand, he pursed his lips thoughtfully. Finally he said, "We'll help you—in return for that little bottle."

"All right," Meg said. "Take us to the best wizard in Crown."

"Right to his doorstep," Dock agreed.

Strangely, Meg felt better with the escort of hoodlums as they made their way through the winding streets and alleys of the night.

"You're not really a witch, are you?" asked Dock when they had stopped in a street where tall dark houses elbowed each other, snatching at starlight.

Meg only smiled.

"What do you want a wizard for, anyway?" he added.

"My best friend's been enchanted," she told him. "I need a counterspell."

Dock nodded approvingly. "Got to stand by your mates."

Meg handed him the invisibility vial, hoping the boys wouldn't make too much trouble with it. "You should know," she warned him, "there's been a bit of invisibility up at the castle. Best keep this a secret."

"Thanks," Dock said. "It's that door." Meg could have guessed at this point. The wizard's house glowed slightly. It was a strange shade of green, with shingles layered down from the roof over onto the walls like the scales of a snake, and a door like a red tongue.

Dock turned to go. Most of the boys followed him, but the smallest one dashed at Meg, his hand making a quick grab at her pocket. Instead of a gold coin, he caught the end of Gorba's scarf.

The scarf shook itself free, diving back into Meg's pocket. The boy ran off as the others laughed. "Maybe you are a witch," Dock said as he led his gang away. Meg marched up the steps and knocked on the wizard's door.

"Honored guests," King Stromgard announced to the gathered princes, "my men are organizing to search the woods." The princes stopped arguing to listen. "I need to know: are your hearts and hands pledged to the rescue of the Princess Margaret?"

The princes cheered, lifting their fists.

"My guard captain will give you your assignments," the king told them.

To one side of the courtyard, Hanak began distributing lanterns and dividing the men into teams for scouring the Witch's Wood. Soon the princes were striding out, tugging their sword belts straight and talking about the hunt before them. At the king's request, the prime minister accompanied them, looking more anxious than usual.

Bain watched the proceedings with interest.

"Do you think she's still there?" Feg asked, sidling up next to him.

"The witch? No."

Vantor was swinging his sword menacingly. When he caught sight of Bain watching him, he stroked one finger along the blade, narrowing his eyes. Bain smiled. "Come on," he said to his man. "I plan to decide what I'm going to do before I do it." He tipped his head in Vantor's direction. "Unlike our ever-so-obvious friend."

Vantor watched Bain depart. "That coward isn't even going to join the search," he said.

"No, Your Highness," his new manservant agreed with a snuffle of his prominent nose.

"Get a group of four or five men to search for her as conspicuously as possible, then meet me down on the road with the others."

"Where are we going?"

Vantor stared at him as if he were stupider than a centipede. "To find the bandits."

No one answered the wizard's door for a long time. Meg and Nort took turns knocking and nursing their sore knuckles. For all the door looked like a tongue, it wasn't soft like a tongue. "Those boys tricked us," Nort grumbled. "It's just an empty house." He rapped once more —and the door swung open with an irate creak. A brownish half-eaten apple floated just in front of them. When they stepped inside, it moved away. "We follow it," Meg concluded.

"Yuck," said Nort.

The entire entry hall seemed as if rust-colored wax had been stopped in the middle of melting. A mirror hung on one blobby wall. When Meg looked in it, she saw herself flickering in and out of sight—as a toddler, a young lady, an eight-year-old, a silver-haired woman. But the apple core was moving, and she pulled herself away.

Their guide led them upstairs and down, through a maze of passageways and doorways until their feet ached. They went into a long hall with varicolored fish swishing past them like birds. Nort touched the air around him, half expecting it to be wet.

Three rooms later they found themselves walking backward through the year—summer into spring into winter into fall. Meg tried not to think about stories she'd heard of widdershins magic. Then the two of them had to crawl down a dark, narrow passageway while the horrible sound of hundreds of tiny feet scritch-scratched around them. Eventually they stood before a door carved with smug-looking mythical beasts. Meg turned the handle and pushed the door open.

By the faint light of a streetlamp she and Nort could see down a grubby flight of steps into a back alley. A strong gust of pepper-scented wind tried to blow them out the door, but Meg grabbed the jamb, sneezing, and Nort caught her hand as he stumbled by, sneezing too. Meg pulled him inside. She fought the wind to slam the door shut, trembling with rage. Nort was still sneezing. Meg sneezed one last time and caught her breath. "We're not going!" she shouted.

They wandered the halls for a while, ignoring the apple core until it gave up and went away. "I've got a blister," Nort said, breaking the discouraged silence.

"Let's rest here." They sat down right where they were, halfway up a flight of ornate jade stairs.

"If he won't see us, there's nothing we can do about it," Nort said.

"We could try making him mad."

"*You're* mad. And I mean the other kind of mad."

"I know what you mean," Meg said haughtily. She pulled out Gorba's scarf and began toying with it. "I don't suppose you're any good at wizard-finding?" she asked it.

The scarf danced into the air.

Meg jumped up. "You are?"

The scarf waved and pointed.

"Why not?" Meg said, following the scarf.

Nort came after her. "Wait for me!"

The scarf led them through what appeared to be the very same endless passageways. "I've seen that painting before," Nort said accusingly, pointing at a portrait of a well-dressed skeleton. "Maybe it's playing a joke on us."

"Maybe," Meg said. But the scarf fluttered on, and she kept walking.

At last the scarf stopped, gesturing frantically at a wooden door half-hidden in the shadows. Meg raised her hand to knock, but the door resolved itself into a long wooden face and spoke irritably. "The wizard already gave to the Widows and Orphans Fund, and you are obviously too poor to be actual customers."

"Don't judge by appearances," Meg said. "Besides, you've got an apple core floating around your fancy house."

"The Golden Apple of Welcoming Delight is reserved for paying guests," sniped the door. It did not open.

"We need a counterspell," Nort tried.

"No," the door said. "Bad for business."

"Why?" Meg asked.

"Because," the door lectured, "the first customer wishes his curse to stick. He does not desire his victims' friends and relations to come around buying a counterspell. If he'd thought that was going to happen, he would have gone to a different wizard. Now, good day to you!" When they didn't move, the door sneered, "By which I mean, go away!"

"What if," Meg said calmly, "the spell missed its intended target and hit an innocent bystander?"

The door looked surprised.

"And what if," Meg went on, "the innocent bystander's friend had a pocket full of dragon gold?"

There was a moment's pause. The door swung open.

13

HE WIZARD WAS VERY SHORT. HE WORE A mask covered with evil-looking runes and gashes like scars. The wizard's great black cloak hid the rest of him, slopping over onto his chair, which was carved with still more baneful runes. This room was ribbed like the insides of a great iron beast. The deep fireplace gaped hungrily. The table and chairs in the corner reminded Meg of thorns. Beside the princess, Nort shivered.

"You're the wizard?" Meg asked.

"I am," said a gruff voice.

Meg came closer. "What's your name?"

"Wizards never tell their names. You may call me Lex."

"That's not a wizardly name," Nort said.

"Ah, but it's *not* my name," Lex said triumphantly. "Now. To business. Let's see this gold of yours. Dragon gold? Truly?"

Meg lifted a handful of treasure from her pocket and displayed it.

"A dragon's treasure has magical properties," the wizard said longingly. "It steeps in dragon magic as the centuries pass."

Meg put the jewels and coins back in her pocket. "The counterspell," she prompted.

"Which spell was it?" Lex asked. "The Terrifying Scourge of Baldness? The Evil Cloud of Itch? Or the Midnight Bark of the Dreaded Neighbor's Dog?"

Meg and Nort looked at each other. "Who names your spells?" Meg asked.

The wizard coughed. "You simple folk cannot comprehend the greatness of wizardly ways and wizardly speech." His voice cracked partway through this pronouncement.

Nort stared. "You're not very old, are you?"

"Lo, I am ancient in years and in wisdom," the wizard proclaimed oracularly. His voice cracked again.

"Are not," Meg said.

The wizard Lex was silent for a moment. Then he drew back his dark hood, uncovering an amazing shock of red hair. He pulled off the mask, revealing a bony boy's face patterned with freckles like a more cheerful sort of rune. His dramatically bushy eyebrows were his only impressive feature. "What gave me away?"

Meg shrugged. "Little things."

The wizard frowned. "I've been practicing and practicing my aura of lordly darkness."

"Maybe in a few years," Meg suggested. "But it must not matter. Everyone knows you're the best."

"That's true. My mother says I'm the most talented wizard in three kingdoms. There's an old wizard on the Isle of Skape who's better, but he's had years to refine his techniques. Which spell are you here about?"

"A glowing ball that turned my friend into a little silver box."

"Triangular?" Lex asked.

"That's the one."

Lex brightened. "Capture Your Enemy for the Indefinite Future. Doubles as a conversation piece."

"What does?"

"The box, of course. It's very pretty."

Meg managed not to roll her eyes. The wizard seemed to have trouble sticking to the point.

Lex hopped to another thought. "Was my client upset?"

"Amused," Meg said. "He threw it and missed."

"Amused. Are you sure?"

Meg nodded.

"After all, the spell did what it was supposed to," the young wizard reflected. "Anyone can see I'm not responsible for customer error. Even a certain sinister dark-haired client would have to admit it."

"Bain," Nort whispered to Meg unnecessarily.

Just then the scarf, which had draped itself around Meg's neck outside the wizard's door, uncoiled and sailed down to the floor. It began crawling about like a midnight-colored serpent. Lex watched, fascinated. "Where did you get that?"

"The witch," Meg told him. "Her grandmother made it."

Lex crouched to get a better look. The scarf slithered away under the thorny table. "What does it do?"

"Whatever it feels like," Nort grumbled.

Meg grinned. "That's true."

Lex stood up again. "I don't suppose you'd like to sell it?"

"It's not mine. It's only borrowed." Besides, Meg thought, the scarf was proving to be far more useful than she had anticipated. Even if it was a bit fickle.

"Pity. My great-aunt made a griffin out of smoke once," Lex remarked.

Nort cleared his throat.

"The counterspell?" Meg said gently.

Lex looked puzzled, but only for a moment. "Yes, yes. You two wait here. Don't touch anything."

"Can't we watch?" Meg said, disappointed.

"Magic is a solitary art," Lex informed her. "Also prone to unfortunate splatters."

He stood, tripping a little over his robes. As if to make up for that, the wizard disappeared in a flash of scarlet light.

"Show-off," said Nort.

Feg paced around the prince's chamber while Bain sat lazily in a carved chair, toying with a tiny silver box on a chain. "Vantor turned purple when I mentioned the bandits might be involved," Bain said.

Feg stopped pacing, surprised. "You saw the tower—didn't see it, I mean," he said. "The witch took the princess."

"Perhaps."

"Vantor's men were muttering about bandits. They'd been out searching for them all day."

"Did they find any?"

Feg laughed.

"He's hoping we'll all go after the witch so he can hunt bandits in peace," Bain observed. "Thinks it's a secret."

"Every man-at-arms for fifty miles around is talking about how the bandits left him tied up on the mountain."

"There's even a lute ballad," Bain said complacently. *"Oh, Vantor went up the dragon's hill, but he only came halfway down,"* the prince sang.

"He has a lot more men now."

"Where did he get them?"

"They say his brother sent most of them. He hired a few more in the worst section of Crown."

"Won't do him any good if he can't find the bandits," Bain remarked. The prince sat up, leaning his chin on his hands. "Me, I want to find that girl."

"What girl?"

"The one at the witch's hut. She knows where the

dragon is. She knows where the witch is. And I've got something she wants." Bain closed his hand around the little box.

"Who is she?"

"I intend to find out." Prince Bain stood up.

"Aren't you going to rescue the princess?"

Bain considered the matter. "Suppose the witch didn't make that spell. Then it would have to be a wizard."

"They'd do it, if the price was right," Feg said.

"One of the other princes might have paid for a spell and kidnapped the princess. To make sure no one else got her out first."

"He could claim to have rescued her later," Feg agreed.

"Vantor doesn't have that much imagination." Bain looked in the wavy glass, smoothing his hair. Next he rumpled it just a little.

"What are you going to do?" Feg asked. "The witch and the girl could be anywhere."

"The rest of that crowd can march around the woods all night. We'll start by asking for information here in the castle. The girl and her friend may have been castle servants."

"We?"

"You'll talk to the stableboys and manservants. I'll talk with the maids and ladies."

Feg guffawed. "Of course you will." He sobered. "It

won't do any good. There must be dozens of servant girls with brown braids."

"Ask the men if they've seen anything odd," Bain told him.

"Maybe she wasn't from the castle at all."

"True enough. But we might turn up other tidbits as we spy about."

Feg still looked doubtful. Bain slapped him on the back. "Don't worry, old friend. We'll ride out in the morning. You can go into the city and talk to wizards, to find out if anyone paid for invisibility magic."

"And you?"

"I'll hunt the witch out toward the moors." Bain smiled. "If I find a bandit along the way, so much the better."

"Careful," Feg said. "Wouldn't want you to end up tied to a tree."

The counterspell was a little wooden box, also triangular. It appeared seamless, but Lex assured them it was not. "Give it a twist, then touch the silver box with it," he said, showing Meg which way to hold the new box.

"All right," Meg said, putting out her hand.

The wizard gave her the box. "My payment?" he said politely.

Meg drew out the dragon gold and piled it on the table. "What do you want all this treasure for?"

Lex gestured around the room. "My fees usually go

toward overhead. Magic costs, you know. Powdered wyvern's tail doubled in price just last month."

"But you said dragon's gold is magic," Nort remembered.

"Even better. I can use most of it directly for my spells."

Meg and Nort moved toward the door.

"Are you sure you wouldn't like to stay and talk a bit?" the young wizard asked, disappointed. "I could make hot chocolate."

Nort perked up at this, but Meg shook her head. "We've got to find out where Bain's keeping the spell."

"That's Dilly's job," Nort said.

"You could sleep over," Lex told them. "I've got guest rooms."

"Bain won't be going anywhere tonight," Nort pointed out. "Even if he does, Dilly can follow him."

Lex looked hopeful.

"It's not like we can sleep in our own beds," Nort said significantly.

Meg felt her own weariness. It *was* rather late. That Bain would probably be going to bed himself. "All right," she said. "But we'll have to get up early." She remembered her manners. "Thank you, Lex."

"You're welcome!" The wizard bustled out of the room, coming back shortly with three steaming mugs of chocolate. Meg hoped he kept his food supplies and his magic supplies separate. Her stomach growled.

Nort turned toward the fireplace, where purple and green flames curled dangerously. "Do you have any marshmallows?"

Lex nodded. "And bread for toasting, too." He flicked his hand. A plate of bread and marshmallows thumped out of thin air onto the table. Three silver toasting forks popped into sight beside them.

"Why didn't you get the chocolate that way?"

"It's liable to spill," Lex explained. He tilted his head quizzically. "Why can't you sleep in your own beds?"

Dilly kept her head down, finishing her work. At last she made her way toward the little room she shared with three other maids, hoping not to have to talk with any of them. She was good at keeping secrets, but they did prickle her insides. I should have pretended I didn't know anything, she told herself, wondering what Meg would think about her encounter with the queen. But the queen had already known Meg was out. And, Dilly thought hopefully, she didn't act like she was going to interfere. Dilly turned a corner.

Prince Bain was in the passageway, talking to Maude, the queen's lady-in-waiting. Dilly turned softly to go back the other way, but they had already seen her.

"That's Dilly," Maude said, "the princess's own maid." Dilly froze.

"Thank you," Bain said charmingly. Maude simpered as he walked toward Dilly. Finally Maude left, with a last longing gaze at the prince.

As Bain came closer, he lifted his brows. "Ah," he said. "You are *also* the young lady I met outside the witch's cottage."

Dilly scowled. "I told you, I went after a love spell!"

"Did you?" The prince lowered his voice, staring at Dilly with his bright eyes. "Or were you there to sell your mistress into the hands of the crone?"

Dilly's jaw dropped. "I would *never*—" she said indignantly, but Bain interrupted her. "Apparently not."

"I have nothing to say to you, sir."

"No," Bain said thoughtfully. "I suppose you don't." He stood watching Dilly as she scurried away down the hall.

"I'm the princess," Meg told the wizard. "I've run away from that stupid contest they're having."

Lex's eyes widened. Then he began to laugh. He didn't stop for some time. His laughter was so cheery that Meg giggled a bit, and even Nort smiled reluctantly.

"This is terrific!" Lex said. "I've run away, too!"

"You have?" Meg asked.

Lex waved his hand around. "Oh, my parents know where I am. I sent them a postcard painting of Crown Market."

"But if they know where you are—" Meg said.

Lex interrupted. "I didn't run away from *them*. I ran away from an apprenticeship."

"Why?" Nort asked.

"Because," Lex explained, "I was apprenticed to a fool who didn't know his eels from his sea dragons."

"I *thought* you were too young to be a real wizard," Nort remarked.

Lex looked surprised. "I know what I'm doing."

"You're not evil, are you?" Meg asked. "All those bloodthirsty symbols on your robes . . ."

"It's my image. People expect a bit of horror." Lex picked up their cups. "More hot chocolate?"

"Please."

"But I want to hear your story," the wizard said. "I didn't know you'd run away."

"Who would tell you?" Nort wondered.

Lex snapped his fingers. Three sparks floated out of the fire. "Go over to the castle and see what's happening," he ordered them. The sparks drifted to the door and fizzed through it, disappearing.

"Nobody knew at first," Meg said. She started recounting the events of the last few weeks, with Nort helping when she left something out.

It was after midnight when most of the princes and guardsmen straggled back into the castle courtyard. None of them had found the slightest sign of the witch or the missing princess. Hanak thanked the princes and told them to get some sleep. "We'll try again early in the morning." Hanak dismissed his own men and went to report to the king.

King Stromgard was reading a book about witches.

"She always seemed harmless," he told his guard captain.

"So is a viper, until you try to catch it," Hanak replied.

" 'Economic development,' indeed," the king said with a snort. "This contest has been nothing but trouble."

"That may be," Hanak said carefully. "Let us recover the princess, and afterward you can consider the next step."

"No one's caught a glimpse of my daughter? Or found a small clue?"

"I'm sorry, Sire. We'll widen our search tomorrow."

"Carry on, then."

"Your Majesty, might I suggest you get some rest?"

"I'm not tired," Stromgard said, his eyes bleak.

14

T WAS STILL DARK OUT WHEN LEX RAPPED ON Meg's door. "You did say five," he said apologetically. This morning he was wearing dark purple robes covered with demon faces. The faces showed their fangs when they saw Meg, but she hardly noticed, and Lex shut the door again.

Meg yawned and stretched. She managed to wash up and put on the clean brown dress Lex had somehow provided. The best thing about the dress was that it had secret pockets. Meg tucked the counterspell into one of them before she rambled off behind her swirling scarf to the room where she had first met the boy wizard.

Nort was already there, eating scrambled eggs.

"Did you sleep well?" Lex asked, pouring Meg a glass of apricot juice.

"Mm-hmm," Meg replied.

"Not me," Lex said brightly. "I stayed up making you a new spell."

"I don't have any more treasure," Meg mumbled.

Lex waved his hand. "It's on the house. It's not every day I get to aid and abet a runaway princess."

Meg drank the juice, waking up a bit more.

"What's the spell for?" Nort asked, his mouth full of egg.

Lex held out a small round object.

"It's a compass," Nort said, unimpressed. "Hanak has one."

"Not just any compass. Ordinary compasses point north."

"Where does this one point?" asked Meg, who was starting to feel more like herself.

"It points at the other spell."

"Cam's spell?"

Lex nodded, setting the spell-compass on the table.

"That's wonderful! No matter where Bain goes, we'll be able to find him!"

"It is pretty wonderful, isn't it?" Lex sighed happily and bit into a muffin.

"It'll save us all kinds of trouble," Nort admitted.

Meg picked the compass up. The little arrow—which appeared to be made of bone—spun and lingered. "What's that way?" Meg asked, pointing in the same direction.

"The castle."

"Where Prince Bain is probably still snoring," Nort said.

"With Cam in a box tucked under his pillow," Meg added.

"My spies came back," Lex said. "Bain was in his room, and the other princes and the guards searched the woods most of the night. The king is angry, and the queen is not."

"She isn't?" said Meg, mystified. "Why not?"

"My spies don't do hidden motives," the wizard said.

"Thank you," Meg told him. She finished her breakfast quickly and stood up to go. Nort stood, too.

"You'll come again, won't you?" Lex asked.

"Of course," Meg told him. "It isn't every day you meet a wizard who makes such good hot chocolate."

"And compasses," Lex reminded her.

"And compasses," Meg said.

Gorba fed the chickens while Janna milked the cows. Then they sat down to a companionable meal of hot porridge.

"Do you think she'll bring him back?" Janna asked.

"Yes," Gorba said after a moment. "The girl's got gumption. Like the girls in my books. Only with more— with more gumption."

"What books?" Janna asked.

The witch turned red. "Just some tales of adventure and romance," she said, her voice dropping on the last word.

"Can I see?"

Gorba looked up at the ceiling. "You really ought to patch that crack."

Janna smiled knowingly. "You've been reading Lady Isabella Comfrey's books, haven't you?"

Gorba's mouth dropped open. "You read them, too?"

"*The Golden Goblet of Love*, *The Perils of Princess Peridot*, *The Capture of a Royal Heart* . . ." Janna recited.

"And *Prince of My Dreams*," Gorba added. "What did you think of that Esmeralda?"

For the next few minutes, Janna nearly forgot her brother's troubles, discussing Esmeralda's disdain for poor Prince Bronzehew.

"You know," Gorba said, "all of my frogs are actually enchanted princes."

Janna's eyes widened. "The—the frogs in my cow pasture?"

Meg and Nort circled around behind the castle from the west. The sky grew lighter as they hurried to meet Dilly.

"Stop!" Nort whispered suddenly.

Meg paused. A mutter of voices reached her from the direction of the pond. She hunched down beside Nort. They began to creep closer.

"She's not likely to be swimming in the frog pond," a man's voice said.

"Vantor ordered us to search out here, so we search out here," someone else rejoined. Meg looked through the edge of a bush at Vantor's men. She gestured at Nort to pull back. They retreated a good thirty paces and hid in a little copse of trees, maneuvering so they could still see the men. "Which way are you going?" the princess muttered as she watched them trample the grass around the pond.

"The other way," Nort said hopefully.

Sure enough, Vantor's men moved east.

"Here comes Dilly," said Nort a moment later, starting to move.

"Wait," Meg told him. "Over there—behind her."

Nort peered at the shadows off to their right. One of them moved. "It's Prince Bain."

Meg took out Lex's little compass. The arrow pointed right at Bain. "He has Cam."

"Let's all three jump on him and take the box!"

"No," Meg said with a great deal of reluctance. Vantor's men were moving away, but they were still within shouting distance. "They'll hear us. Besides, he has a knife. I don't want you and Dilly getting hurt."

"Or you," Nort pointed out.

"I'd rather steal it from him."

"So what are we going to do?"

"I have a better question," Meg said as Dilly reached the pond and stopped, looking around. "Why is he following Dilly?"

"He did see her at the witch's house."

"She told him she was there for a love spell," Meg said, thinking.

Nort nodded.

"Dilly must be meeting her sweetheart down by the frog pond."

"What?" Nort stared at Meg, confused.

"That's what Bain should think, anyway."

Nort shrugged. "What are you talking about?"

"*You're* going to be her sweetheart."

"What!" Nort said again, so loudly that Meg had to shush him.

"Something's wrong. Maybe this will make him less suspicious. And it will make it easier for me to follow him," Meg explained.

"I should come with you!"

Meg waited stubbornly.

Nort made a face. "But Dilly won't know," he argued.

"Whisper it in her ear," Meg suggested.

Nort's brows lowered, but he said nothing. He merely crawled off through the underbrush toward the castle. When he was out of sight of both Dilly and Bain, he stood and walked back toward the frog pond.

Meg had a more difficult task, shadowing the shadow. She crept behind the hidden prince and waited. It helped that he was distracted by the sight of Nort coming over the hill. When Nort had passed, Bain went after him toward the pond. Meg followed Bain with careful movements. He glanced back once, but she froze, and he moved on.

Nort strode down to the pond, lifting his finger to his lips in front of him, where Bain couldn't see.

Dilly swallowed the words she had been about to say.

Nort came right up to her and stood too close. "Bain's watching," he muttered.

"I see. Where's . . . ?" Dilly left off the name.

"Nearby. I'm to pretend I'm the boy you were getting the love spell for."

"What?" Dilly said loudly. "Oh." In a false voice, she went on, "Nort, how I've waited and waited for you."

Nort took her hand, gritting his teeth. "How beautiful you look this morning," he announced.

With an effort, the two embraced. Still Bain waited. Turning her eyes slantways, Dilly could just see his hair behind the reeds.

"When are you going to tell your father and mother about us?" Nort inquired.

"Soon, my dearest," Dilly replied in lilting tones.

"Your eyes are so very blue," Nort told her.

"Yours, too," said Dilly. Bain's hair was no longer visible. In a lower voice, she said, "Do you think that's enough?"

Nort looked up the hill toward the castle. "I hope so," he breathed. "I must get back to work, my sweet," he said, raising his voice again.

They started back at a leisurely pace, in case the prince was still lurking about and needed to get out of their way.

"Why was he following you?" Nort whispered.

"Later," Dilly said.

They walked in silence for a moment. Then Dilly asked smarmily, "Do you really think my eyes are blue?"

"It's a simple fact," Nort snapped. "Come on."

"I think you've forgotten something."

"What?"

"You can't be seen at the castle," Dilly reminded him.

Nort flushed. "If I hurry, maybe I can catch up with Meg."

Dilly trailed him around the castle toward the stables.

After listening to Dilly and Nort exchange a few sweet nothings, Bain had crept up the hill again, surprising Meg, who hadn't considered his return path. She ended up flinging herself flat on the ground behind a too-short bush. Meg could hear the wind in the grass, the murmur of her friends' voices, and there—soft footsteps coming very near. She held her breath. The steps passed by.

Meg remembered abruptly that only three days ago she and Cam had spied on Bain together, hiding in the grass just like this. She lifted her head. Bain was walking back toward the castle.

Meg followed him around the west side, grateful it was so early that few of the castle folk were about. Bain stopped at the stables and spoke to a groom. The princess waited in the shadows. "No," she said, aghast. He was going on horseback!

Sure enough, the groom brought out Bain's horse.

Meg had to watch Bain leap gracefully into the saddle and ride away down the royal road to the east.

Meg took the spell-compass out and consoled herself by watching its arrow turn in Bain's direction. "I *will* catch up to you," she promised. She touched the counterspell in her other pocket. She was going to need a horse of her own.

As if in answer, the groom led out a second horse and tethered it to a post. The stallion snorted, tossing his head. Meg's eyes gleamed. Hanak had always put her on placid mares, despite her protests. "You'll do," she murmured to her soon-to-be mount as the obliging groom stepped into the stable. Meg ran and quickly untied the horse's reins. To the horse's surprise, she managed to clamber onto his back. The horse bucked. Somehow she kept her seat, pulling the stallion's head around.

The groom came running out. "Hey!" he yelled as Meg burst down the hill onto the road east, taking the same path as the black-haired prince. "Black-hearted," she spat, clinging to the horse as it galloped wildly away.

Dilly and Nort peeped around the corner just in time to see Meg's departing back. They watched Prince Vantor come striding out to the stables seconds later. "Where's my horse?" he demanded. But the groomsman could only shake his head and point at the tiny figure in the distance.

Dilly and Nort prudently withdrew as Vantor's shouts echoed through the stable yard.

"I should have gone with her," Nort said.

"So now what will you do?"

"I can't stay here," Nort said, remembering he was a wanted man.

"Spy on Vantor."

"He's right there!"

"Yes, but everyone knows he's after the bandits. You can follow him."

Nort looked at Dilly as if she were crazy.

"Do what you want," she said. "I've got to get back to work." And she flounced off.

Nort's stomach complained. He had to tell himself not to go to the kitchen to beg some toast from the cook. Instead he slunk away from the stables and took a circuitous route to the royal road. Then he set out after Meg. If he couldn't find her, maybe he could become a bandit, Nort thought miserably. He found himself wondering if there was a price on his head, and whether the balladeers might have anything to say about that.

The twin princes of Hanaby Keep had brought enough supplies up the mountainside for a week, which was just as well, since it might take that long to complete the dragon trap. Once the pit had been thoroughly dug, Dagle started chopping trees for the trapping mechanism while Dorn scribbled engineering plans on scraps of parchment.

"What we need is a spring-loaded device," Dorn told his brother over their lunch of cake and dried fruit.

"Like a giant mousetrap?" Dagle asked.

"Much more elaborate," Dorn said proudly. "As befits the wiles of a dragon."

"Not to mention our wiles." Dagle took another bite of cake.

To one side of their camp, the cow tugged again and again against the tree, catching a predatory scent on the wind. She mooed plaintively.

"What's wrong with her?" Dorn asked, glancing over.

"Maybe she needs to be milked," Dagle said. "Go check."

"You check."

"No, you check."

"We'll do it together," Dorn concluded. The princes approached the animal and examined her udder.

"I don't think that's it," Dagle said.

Dorn shrugged. "Maybe she knows what we've got planned for her."

"Maybe," Dagle said. "Come on. I think we've got enough wood."

Northwest of Greeve, a messenger rode up to the palace gates of the Kingdom of Tarylon. His exhausted mount was led to the stables, and the messenger himself was brought before the king. Most days King Tark of Tarylon looked a lot like his son, with rumpled brown hair and an easy smile. Today, however, he was not smiling.

The king accepted the leather pouch from the messenger, extracting a parchment scroll from within. He read it. His frown deepened into an ominous scowl. "So," he said, "Stromgard of Greeve thinks to hold our sons by his enchantments." King Tark leaped to his feet. "Call my generals!" he ordered. He remembered the courier. "I've a message for your master."

15

T FIRST MEG RODE AS HARD AS SHE COULD, thudding past early-rising marketgoers in a wild blur. She still couldn't catch sight of Prince Bain, and the horse began to pant and pull. Meg slowed the horse to a trot. She cupped the compass in her hand, reminding herself that the prince couldn't escape its needle.

Meg had soon passed the waking city of Crown and was riding through the southern stretch of the Witch's Wood (Gorba's wood, she thought). The people she passed eyed her curiously. Only one spoke, a sturdy-looking farmer driving a cart filled with beets. He tipped his hat, and Meg smiled. Then he asked, "Where'd you get that horse, lass?" Meg rode on without answering.

After the woods finally faded, farms ran along both sides of the road. Meg thought wistfully of Janna and Gorba to her north, at Hookhorn Farm. But it would do no good to go back without Cam, and she kept riding.

She was nearly to the moors when her thirst overcame her, and she realized belatedly that the horse needed water, too. Meg walked the stallion up to the fence of the last farmhouse to see if she could water him there.

"Hello!" Meg called, tying the horse to the fence post.

There was no answer. For that matter, there was no sign of life, now that she looked closely. The fence was leaning as if it wanted to fall down altogether. There were no curtains at the windows of the house.

"Let's hope the well's not dry," she told the horse, who had already busied himself cropping weeds.

The well was behind the house. The winch and chain appeared fine, if a little rusty, and the bucket was intact. Meg cleared a growth of morning glories away from the well's mouth and struggled to lift the worn well cover. When it came loose, the wooden wheel nearly landed on her foot, but she heaved it aside, leaning it against the well.

Meg reached for a pebble and dropped it into the darkness. It landed far below with a dry *thwick*. "Huh," Meg said, wiping her brow. "After all that work!"

She felt a rustling in her pocket. The scarf poked one corner out and stared about with several of its beady eyes.

The land sloped away gradually from the back of the farmhouse, ending in a line of brighter green. "That will be water!" Meg told the scarf. She went down the hill to see. Sure enough, a stream ran through the pastures, crowded by thirsty grasses and trees. Really, it was nearly wide enough to be a small river. Meg knelt, cupping her hands to drink. Then she went back up the hill to fetch her horse, wondering as she went why the farmer had abandoned such a pretty place.

Meg came around the corner of the farmhouse and stopped short. Vantor's men were there. *Vantor* was there, pulling on the stallion's reins. All of them turned to look at Meg.

"Thief!" the prince shouted, pointing. The horse took advantage of the situation to bolt.

A fraction of a second later, Meg was pelting back toward the stream with what seemed like a small army pounding after her.

Meg hit the banks and plowed right into the water. The men kept coming. She felt a tug at her hip as she hurried across, trying not to slip on the stones beneath her feet. She was going too fast, though, and she fell, drenching herself. She jumped up again instantly and struggled on.

There were only two men, as it turned out. Vantor didn't count, standing on the bank watching other people get their clothes wet.

The first man splashed after Meg, already too near. She turned and slapped a good sluice of water up his beak of a nose. He fell back coughing, but the other man, a big black-haired thug, grabbed Meg's arm. She twisted free and punched him in the face as hard as she could.

Apparently, he hadn't expected that: his surprise gave Meg a fraction of a second to gain on him. The man threw his huge body at her, roaring like a bear. Meg shoved herself toward the opposite bank, barely out of his reach as he fell facedown in the water. Beaknose was moving again, and behind him Vantor was hollering helpfully on the farmhouse side of the water. "Get her, you fools! Get her!"

Meg reached in her pocket without thinking, wishing she had a knife or a box of pepper—*anything*. Gorba's scarf came out in her hand instead, so she flipped it hard at Beaknose's protruding snout. The scarf shrieked like nothing Meg had ever heard before and latched onto the man's nose. Meg let go of the other end, backing away as he fought to tear it off. Finally the scarf loosened its hold and flew after Meg, undulating horribly. Meg made for land at top speed. The man howled. She stole another glance behind her. His nose looked as if it had run into a hornet's nest. Meg climbed up the bank.

"Witch!" Beaknose shouted, but he had stopped following her. Bear, who had gotten up and begun to surge after her, slowed, his angry eyes turning uncertain. Behind him, Vantor closed his mouth abruptly.

If they were scared of her, maybe they'd let her go. "That's right!" Meg taunted. "I turned your Horace into a salamander!" She ran, with the scarf flapping about her like an addled bird. If she hadn't known it was on her side, she would have been frightened by it.

Meg ran down hills and up hills, around thick stands

of trees and through thin, snatching brambles. She
didn't stop until she had to. She stood still for a moment, panting. "Thank you," she said to the scarf when
she had caught her breath. She examined it carefully as it
glided closer, but she couldn't see any teeth or stingers.
Just those eyes.

The scarf draped itself around Meg's shoulders. She
tried not to shiver as its lashes tickled her neck. The scarf
waited expectantly. Meg collected herself, remembering
Lex's compass. She drew it out of her other pocket. The
bone arrow spun, then steadied, pointing. "This way,"
Meg said to her strange companion as she marched between the bushes, hoping her clothes would dry soon.

"What was that thing?" Vantor asked.

"A lady's scarf," the big man said.

"It bit me!" moaned the other, still nursing his nose.

"Then it flew away," Vantor said thoughtfully. "You
were right."

The men gawked. The prince had never said such a
thing before.

"A witch can take any form she wants," Vantor went
on. "What better disguise than the shape of a harmless
girl?"

"And the scarf was her familiar!" the wounded man
cried, hoping his cleverness would be rewarded.

"Perhaps," the prince said. "Which means we had
one of the prizes we're seeking in our hands, and you let
her go."

Bear and Beaknose looked at each other unhappily. It seemed Beaknose's cleverness was going to be punished.

"She won't have gone far. Find her. Bring her to the meeting place."

"Meeting place?" Bear repeated.

"On the moors? The very large oak tree where I divided you into groups just last night in order"—Vantor sucked a breath between his teeth—"to search for bandits? The bandits we're *looking* for?"

"The secret camp," Bear said, pleased.

"What about the witch's familiar?" Beaknose asked before Vantor could explode.

Vantor waved a dismissive hand. "Now that you're warned, you can deal with it."

Beaknose didn't look convinced, but he held his peace. Just then another of Vantor's men came down the hill from the house.

"Well?" the prince demanded.

The man shook his head. "He got away." Vantor's face tightened, and the man added hastily, "We still have your other horse!"

"Miserable beast. The castle should have given me its best mount." Vantor pulled a bag of coins from his pocket. "Ride into town. Get me a real horse."

The guardsman took the coins and hurried away.

"Where are you going, Your Highness?" Beaknose managed to ask.

Vantor strode off without answering.

"He'll be hunting those bandits again," said Bear. "And our gold."

"*His* gold," Beaknose muttered, wringing the water out of his sleeves.

Nort trudged along the royal road, wondering whether Meg had stayed on it for long, but uncertain where to turn if she had not. He passed a throng of farm folk heading to market, but he kept his head down and didn't meet their eyes. He'd been walking at least an hour when someone surprised him by stepping in front of him, blocking his way. Nort looked up.

"Young Nort," Hanak said ominously. Half a dozen guardsmen waited behind him.

Nort felt his head spinning. "Yes, sir," he managed.

"Where might you be going?"

"To find the princess, sir." That at least was true.

Hanak smiled, but it was not a kind smile. "Coincidentally enough, we've been searching for her as well."

Nort peered past Hanak at the other guardsmen. He knew them all. In the past they had sometimes given him advice or even praise. Now none of them looked friendly.

"I'm thinking," Hanak said, "that your disappearance means one of two things. Either you had something to do with the princess being gone—"

"Oh no, sir! I would never!" Nort babbled. He fell silent, realizing he'd interrupted the captain. "Sorry, sir."

"Or," Hanak continued, "you're a coward."

Nort shook his head.

"At any rate, I've already got my orders concerning you."

Nort waited, puzzled.

"I believe the king's exact words were 'And if you find the idiot who was guarding her, throw him in the dungeons.'"

Nort gasped. The rest of the guards snickered.

"Come along," Hanak said. "You can tell me your version of what happened as we march."

Nort turned back toward the castle, wishing he had a choice in the matter.

"Was it that witch?" the captain asked.

Lying had always come easily to Nort. But today he discovered it was much more difficult to lie while imagining the dungeons under the castle. I could tell the truth, he thought, but then he pictured Meg's face, pictured her saying to the others, "I knew we shouldn't have trusted him." She'll come back and sort this all out, he assured himself as he launched into a tale that started with the witch and soon soared into an epic adventure involving flying trolls and conspiracies among the southern kings.

When he had finished, Nort abruptly recalled his audience. From the expression on Hanak's face, Nort knew the captain didn't believe a word of his story. The company walked the rest of the way to the castle and through the courtyard in silence. The other men dispersed while

Hanak led Nort silently down the dark stairs into the belly of the castle.

It wasn't nearly as nice traveling on foot, Meg decided. For one thing, she was already footsore from all the tromping around she'd been doing the last few days. For another, it seemed like every briar and rock in Greeve conspired to be in her path as she followed the compass needle toward Bain and his prisoner. Besides which, her only companion was a magic scarf, and it kept wandering off.

Meg came to a swampy stretch after a bit and had to take the time to consider whether she was stepping on solid ground as she negotiated the bright hummocks of grass and circled equally green pools of algae. The mosquitoes welcomed her with gusto. The frog song that stopped when she came near made her wish Gorba were with her. Meg glanced up at the scarf—and fell into a deep pool. She sank fast and flailed, rising up coughing brackish water, soaked for the second time today.

"Help!" she cried out of reflex. There was no one to hear her. The scarf, busy chasing a bee, didn't notice her predicament.

Meg grabbed at clumps of grass, but her wet hands slipped off and she went back under the water.

If it hadn't been for Cam teaching her to swim in the frog pond, she would have drowned. As it was, Meg managed to paddle a little and reach the edge of the pool again. She slid along until she finally found a patch of roots that held when she pulled on them. Slowly Meg dragged her body up and out of the water.

She lay on the ground for a long while, panting and covered in marsh slime. Then she stood to wring out her skirt and slog onward, trying not to be angry with Cam for getting himself turned into a box. Meg shivered despite the late afternoon sunlight. Her clothes dried eventually, but they felt stiff and itchy. Her mosquito bites itched even more.

The princess laughed. She had wanted to get out of the castle and go on a grand adventure, but now that she was in the middle of it, she was very uncomfortable. The scarf circled inquiringly overhead. "Don't worry," Meg told it. "I'd still rather be here than locked in that heap of stones."

She walked on, more careful now. The sun began to sink, and the swamp ended. Meg hiked along a grassy hill dotted with shrubs and trees. Already feeling more cheerful, she came across a patch of raspberries not five minutes later and brightened still more. She sat down to rest her sore feet and eat berries.

"I thought you said you could track anything," Bear said.

"I *am* tracking," Beaknose answered tightly.

Bear kicked a rock. "Anything but a little witch, eh?"

Beaknose stomped on. "There," he said, pointing at a bush. "See that twig? She broke that."

"Or a fox did, or a rabbit, or a—"

"Shut up!"

Bear smirked, following his shorter companion. "Or a hedgehog, or a deer—could have been a baby deer or a mama deer—"

"I can't track with you yammering on like that," Beak-nose growled.

Bear fell silent. A wolf, a squirrel, even an opossum, he thought, lumbering on.

When Meg opened her eyes, it was dark. "Scarf!" Meg cried. "I didn't mean to fall asleep! Why didn't you wake me?" Something tickled her cheek. "Oh. You did." Meg struggled to her feet.

For a moment she was afraid she wouldn't be able to see Lex's compass in the starlight, but the boy wizard had thought of that, too: the compass glowed softly, like a small moon.

It'll be easier to sneak up on that fool prince at night, Meg told herself as she went on, trying not to trip in the darkness. She could only hope Bain had stopped for the night. He hadn't gone back to the castle; the compass proved that.

Sometime later, Meg came over a hill and saw a faint flicker through the trees below her. Beyond the trees lay the moors, vast and dark. She watched for a moment, until she was sure she was seeing the light of a fire. Bain, she thought exultantly. Meg crept downward. As she came closer to the fire, she heard voices. Someone walked by her to the left, and she froze. Who were all these people? Bain had been alone when he left the castle.

But the compass drew her on. Cam would be just ahead of her. The counterspell rested in the bottom of her hidden pocket, ready to save her friend.

Meg moved from one tree to the next, using her hand to shield the light of the compass from strange eyes. Then someone grabbed her from behind and she yelled, dropping the compass. The scarf flapped away, startled.

"Who are you, tippy-toeing into our camp?" a rough voice asked. Meg's captor dragged her toward the fire. What would Prince Bain say?

Meg's hands were released. At first she could only blink around at the circle of scowling faces. Then someone was asking a question, and she focused on a young woman with tousled black hair who was saying, "How did you find this place?"

But Meg scarcely heard. She was staring at the woman's throat, where, suspended from a silver chain, lay a small, triangular box.

16

N A CITY NORTH OF GREEVE, KING JAL OF LORS leaned forward, addressing his advisers over the long, candlelit table. "Tark proposes an alliance."

His most senior adviser spoke. "If Tarylon's news is reliable, tell us: what does King Stromgard have to gain by this move?"

"By holding our sons hostage?" King Jal said bitterly. "He would have Lors and Tarylon by their throats."

"And who knows how many other kingdoms?" a general put in, his eyes gleaming.

The king of Lors turned his own eyes to meet the general's and nodded slowly. "We'll leave part of our forces here."

"We?" the senior adviser asked.

"I'm going after my son," said King Jal.

Nort languished. At least, that's what the balladeers always called it. It seemed a lot like feeling sorry for yourself, Nort realized.

The walls were dank stones, and somewhere something dripped not quite often enough that Nort remembered it would, and then every time it did he was annoyed all over again. At least Hanak hadn't bothered to put manacles on him. Why, Nort could walk right from one side of the cell to the other! He tried it. Four short steps or three long ones. He sighed and sat down on the rickety cot, wrapping himself in a piece of burlap that must once have been a feed bag and was now intended to serve as a blanket.

Somewhere nearby, another prisoner was snoring. Whoever it was sounded like he had a bad cold. It was dark down here, and growing darker. "The Loyal Guardsman." That's what his ballad should be called. Nort swiped away a tear, wondering what Meg was doing.

His mouth felt dry. Nort looked around for water. There was a bowl in one corner. It reminded him of a dog dish. Nort tasted the water. It was stale, but he was very thirsty.

Soon he heard footsteps and voices. A light brightened the dimness, coming closer. Not Meg already, Nort thought.

King Stromgard swept to a regal stop in front of Nort's cell and spoke to him through the bars. "Well? What do you have to say for yourself?"

"I'm sorry, Sire," Nort said. Sorry for all kinds of reasons, he thought bitterly.

"What happened?"

Hanak stepped forward beside the king. "And no more cockamamie stories."

"It was magic," Nort told them.

"That much is obvious," the king snapped. "But who did it, and where have they taken my daughter?"

Nort shook his head. "I don't know where she is."

"Did you see who took her?" Hanak asked.

"No."

"Gracklebacks!" the king swore. "Either you're so stupid I can't imagine why we ever took you on, or you're in collusion with the kidnapper."

"Come, Sire," Hanak said. "Perhaps he'll remember something useful tomorrow." The guard captain gave Nort a cold blue look.

"He'd better," said His Majesty, turning away. "Or he'll grow a very long beard before he gets out."

The light faded up the passageway. Nort fingered his chin, trying to remember why he should keep covering for the princess.

It came back to him half an hour later, when Dilly brought him his supper. "Nort?"

He wiped away a few more tears as he sat up. "Dilly?"

She held a candle in one hand and a steaming dish in the other. "Hungry?"

Nort nodded. Dilly scooted the dish under the lower edge of the bars and fished a spoon out of her pocket.

"I don't suppose . . ." Nort's voice trailed off.

"I can't get you out," she said. "But Meg will." She handed him the spoon.

"Is she back?"

"Not yet."

"What if something happened to her?"

"Don't say that." Dilly lifted her candle, frowning. "I *can* bring you a better blanket. And some fresh water."

"Thank you," Nort said.

"You're welcome." Dilly turned to go.

Nort felt panic rising in his throat. "Wait!" he blurted. She looked back. "Can't you stay and talk a little?"

Dilly hesitated. Then she sat down gingerly in the passageway, setting the candle beside her. "Tell me how they caught you."

"Now what?" Bear whispered.

Beside him, Beaknose looked down at the people gathered around the fire. "The witch *and* the bandits? Vantor might give us a little of that gold when he sees this."

"He told us to bring her to him."

Beaknose sighed. "Do us no good to get caught by that bunch."

"He *said*," Bear insisted.

"He also said to report any sign of the bandits' camp."

Bear thought this over. "All right."

The two henchmen went back the way they came. A moment later, one of the bandit sentries passed right where they had been standing, but all she found was leaves.

"Most prisoners are more attentive when we discuss their fates," the woman seated by the fire said dryly.

Meg started. "I beg your pardon?"

"What are you staring at?" the woman asked.

"That little box," Meg admitted out of desperation. "Where did you get it?"

"Ah." The woman touched the trinket at her throat. "You've seen it before?"

Meg nodded, finally looking the woman in the face. The woman was very pretty, with clever green eyes. Suddenly Meg knew where she was. "You—are you a bandit? Where's Bold Rodolfo?"

The woman laughed. "Some call me that, but they have never met me. My own people call me the Bandit Queen. And you have stumbled into our lair." Now her eyes grew watchful. "How did you find us?" she repeated.

"The box—" Meg said, confused. "But Prince Bain had it."

"Not anymore." All of them laughed this time, nudging each other. Meg looked around the circle of faces. They had a hint of the wild about them, the wary expressions of animals in the woods when they catch sight of humans. The bandits were dressed in dark, dull colors, here and there brightened by what must have been stolen rings and earrings and satin scarves.

"So many princes wandering about," their leader mused. "Such kind folk, willing to share their good fortune with the people of Greeve."

"But the princes are after you," Meg said.

"And we're after them," a red-haired man hooted.

The Bandit Queen smiled. "Someone is always after us. In fact, how do we know you haven't come spying for one of those princes? Or the king? And what do you want with this?" The woman touched the box again.

"It's my friend," Meg blurted. "He's been enchanted."

"And I'm the lost princess," one of the bandit girls called. "Tell us another!"

The queen changed the subject abruptly. "Have you eaten?"

Meg shook her head. Suddenly it seemed she hadn't eaten in days. She ached and itched. And worst of all, she could see Cam, but she couldn't save him. Not yet, anyway. Meg tried to collect her courage.

"Lute, get her a bite of supper," the woman commanded. A slender boy jumped up from the fire and went into the darkness.

"Now," the Bandit Queen said, "let's hear your story. Then I'll decide what to do with you."

Meg hesitated. She couldn't tell them who she really was. But she could offer up the pieces of her adventures that had to do with Cam's predicament.

"Thinking of lies?" the woman asked, amused.

"Thinking which parts of the truth might matter to you," Meg said bluntly. "It started when Cam and I went to the witch's cottage."

"Why would you want to go there?" a stout bandit with a beard called. He took a great bite of a pork rib.

"To warn her about the contest."

The Bandit Queen gave her followers a cynical look.

"It's true!" Meg said indignantly. "What's she ever done to anyone, to have the king treat her like that? And all those ridiculous princes, parading around like they own half the kingdom already?" Her hands clenched into fists.

"Hear, hear!" cried an old man.

The Bandit Queen raised her eyebrows. "Not a fan of royalty, are we?"

"She's practically one of us," a woman teased from beyond the flickering flames.

"Go on," said the Bandit Queen.

Meg squashed her anger, returning to her tale. "Anyway, we were trying to warn her when that Bain showed up."

"Another horrid prince," the queen said in placid tones.

"Right. And he threw a spell at the witch, but he missed and hit my friend instead, and when Cam turned into a little silver box, the prince took him and ran away!"

Somebody snorted. "Why would a man like Bain run from the likes of you?"

"Gorba was about to turn him into a frog."

"I see," said the Bandit Queen, sounding as if she did.

"So I was trying to find Bain, and now I'm here," Meg said, jumping to the end of the story. "To get my friend back," she added, in case the bandits weren't clear about that part.

"Which still doesn't explain how you found us, especially as you claim to have been searching for the prince who stole your friend." Murmurs of agreement came from all around.

"I—had a spell."

"Another spell? Show me."

"I lost it in the bushes when your guard grabbed me."

Some of the bandits called out derisively, but the Bandit Queen simply signaled to one of her men. Just then Lute came back with a bowl of something that smelled wonderful. "You may eat while Targel finds the spell," the queen told Meg. "What shape is it?"

"Like a compass, small and round and flat."

Targel went off to look for the spell. Meg dug her spoon ravenously into the dish of meat and vegetables. Some of the other bandits finished eating and departed, but the queen stayed by the fire, talking in a low voice to one of her lieutenants.

Meg watched the Bandit Queen between bites. She

couldn't help admiring the woman a little. The bandit was strong and brave and living just the kind of adventure Meg had always dreamed of having. The adventure involved more dirt than Meg had imagined, and there was the whole problem of stealing, but Meg found herself wondering what it would be like to be a bandit queen instead of the ordinary, stuck-in-a-castle kind.

Despite her daydreaming, Meg managed to finish her food before Targel came back and dropped the spell-compass into his leader's hand. The Bandit Queen turned it in the firelight. "It's beautiful. Where did you get it?"

"I can't tell you all my secrets," Meg said.

"That's wizard work," the queen's lieutenant whispered. He was a twitchy sort, like a young rabbit.

"Witches and wizards," said the Bandit Queen, tossing the compass in the air and catching it. "There's more to your story than you've told."

Meg waited.

"What will you give me for the enchanted box?" the woman asked.

"The compass?" Meg said, knowing it wouldn't be enough.

"I already have it. Besides, its usefulness would appear to have ended." The Bandit Queen moved the compass in a circle around the box at her throat, watching the needle spin frantically to point at Cam's spell. She stopped, leaning forward suddenly. "Perhaps a few of your secrets might be more valuable."

Meg glanced around at the circle of eyes gleaming in the firelight. "I'll tell you some secrets." She looked right at the Bandit Queen and tried to match her boldness. "Just you."

The Bandit Queen laughed. "A woman-to-woman talk, is it? Very well. Come on." She stood up. One of her men instantly handed her a lantern.

Meg gave her bowl to the nearest bandit and followed the Bandit Queen across the camp to a quiet spot. "Pull up a rock," the woman ordered.

Meg plopped down on one rock as the bandit sat on another. "What else do you want to know?" Meg asked.

"I want to know where you got enough money to buy a spell from a first-class wizard," the woman said, toying with Lex's compass again.

"What if I want to know something, too?" Meg dared to say.

"Such as?"

"What's it like to be a bandit queen?" Meg propped her chin on her hands.

"Considering going into the business?"

"Maybe."

The Bandit Queen smiled. "It helps to know how to use a sword. You look more like the embroidery type."

"I do not!" Meg cried so loudly that everyone within sight of them turned to look.

The Bandit Queen's hand had gone to her dagger. "Don't you know it's dangerous to yell at a bandit?" the woman said, relaxing again.

"Sorry," Meg said. "It's just that I *want* to learn to use a sword, and they won't let me."

"Who's 'they'?" the Bandit Queen asked too casually.

Meg was just as careful with her answer. "My father."

"Your rich father?"

"Just my father." Meg could tell the bandit was still trying to find out about the expensive compass spell. "I paid for the spell with dragon gold, all right? I took the gold when no one was watching."

The Bandit Queen looked surprised. Then she smiled slowly. "It seems we have something in common: an interest in dragon's treasure." She tucked the magic compass inside her shirt. "But you are less fortunate than I when it comes to your father. My father taught me swordplay, just as his father taught him. My grandfather was a knight, you see."

"But a knight wouldn't—" Meg stopped herself.

"Wouldn't steal? This one did. Not all stories have happy endings, you know."

"I suppose not. What happened?"

The Bandit Queen shook her head. "Stories are secrets. You must tell me another one first." She seemed to be enjoying this.

Meg cheerfully swiped her friend's identity. "I'm one of the castle maids. My name is Dilly." The bandit didn't seem very impressed. "I could tell you what the princess is like," Meg offered.

"The princess? Do you know where she is?"

"No," Meg said, resisting the urge to cross her fingers.

"Try again."

Meg thought fast. "I could tell you about Prince Vantor. He's one of the princes here for the contest, but he's a liar and a cheat. He was stealing the dragon's treasure, but then—"

"I know all about that," the bandit said smugly. "I stole the treasure from Vantor."

"Ha!" Meg said, in spite of herself.

"Ha indeed. I see I shall have to take pity on you and tell you about my grandfather the knight. He was young and fearless, and he came questing to Greeve, hoping to win the heart of a fair princess."

Meg tried not to make a face. This wasn't her favorite sort of story. "Really?"

"Really. He faced the dreadful dragon of Greeve, with its vast blue scales and its forty-foot flames, but he was too late." The Bandit Queen lowered her voice dramatically on the last few words.

"Why is that?" Meg asked.

"The dragon ate the fair princess before my grandfather could save her."

"Ugh," Meg said. This story was undoubtedly about her great-aunt.

"Ugh indeed. My grandfather was heartbroken, and, as often happens in these cases, he turned to a life of crime." The bandit didn't seem at all sorry about that development.

Meg thought of something else. "Doesn't it bother you that people call you Bold Rodolfo and not—Bold Whatever?"

"Bold Alya?"

Meg repeated the name. "Bold Alya."

The Bandit Queen—Alya—frowned. "The people of Greeve find it easier to imagine a man leading my people." She shrugged. "It allows me a certain amount of freedom." Alya picked up the lantern and got to her feet. "So, Dilly, now that you have seen a little of our lives, eaten our food, and heard our stories, do you still long to be a bandit?"

Meg stood, too. "I want to be the Bandit Queen."

Alya stepped back in mock alarm. "A pretender to my throne!" She touched the rock she'd been sitting on with her foot. "Such a fine throne, encrusted with diamonds and pearls."

Meg half curtsied. "I have a throne as well," she said, indicating her own rock.

"Perhaps when I retire," Alya said. "Which I believe will happen shortly, thanks to an arrogant prince and a certain dragon."

"Retire?" That sounded boring to Meg. "What would you do?"

Alya looked wistful for a moment. "I'd buy land to the south, maybe even on the Isle of Skape. It's very beautiful there."

"And—bandit some more? Just a little?"

"No. Fish, maybe, except that the smell might be too

much, day after day. I could keep bees. Honey's nice. I suppose I'll think of something." The Bandit Queen turned brisk. "Now. I've decided we can work out a payment plan for your silvery friend here. But I'm curious to know how you intend to turn him back."

"I have a counterspell," Meg admitted.

Alya scowled. "My men should have found it when they caught you."

"In a hidden pocket," Meg said placatingly.

"Ah." Alya grinned. "You'd make a very good bandit, young Dilly." Then she lifted her head. "Something's wrong."

Meg listened, but she couldn't hear anything. "What is it?"

Alya drew her dagger and ran across the camp without answering, but she was too late. Men were already pouring down the hillside, yelling hoarsely.

Meg panicked. She raced away from the attackers, but then she heard a woman shriek behind her as if she had been struck by a sword or an arrow. Meg looked back, afraid it was Alya. In the dim light, all she could see was a light-haired bandit struggling with a large man. The big man looked like Bear.

Meg ran again, trying to escape the yelling and fighting. She had nearly reached the trees when another man stepped into her path. "Oh no you don't," he said.

Meg tried ducking around him, but the man menaced her with his sword and she faltered. He grabbed her arm and marched her to the center of the camp, where a number of bandits were huddled together, guarded by several men. In the firelight, Meg could see that their captors' gray tunics were trimmed with blue and gold—Vantor's colors. Children blinked, wide-eyed, clinging to their mothers' skirts. A baby cried on and on.

Vantor's guards built up the fire again, laughing and talking.

Meg kept her head down, hoping for the best, but a hand grabbed her shoulder and spun her around. "You!" Beaknose squawked.

Nort's second royal visitor came well after midnight. "Wake up, young man," a voice said. Nort sat up. The queen was gazing through the bars at him, with Dilly standing beside her.

"Dilly?" Nort asked. He scrambled to his feet and stepped to the front of the cell.

"I understand you've been gallivanting around with my daughter," Queen Istilda said.

Nort looked at Dilly. Dilly nodded slightly.

"Yes, Your Majesty," he stammered.

"Where is she now?"

"She—she was going out to the moors to rescue Cam. On a horse."

"And she hasn't returned."

Nort shook his head. "I don't think so. I was on my way to find her when—"

"When you met up with Hanak," the queen said.

"Yes, Your Majesty."

"And your quest was interrupted," Meg's mother said, watching him closely.

"That's right."

The queen grasped the bars. "Young man, I believe you should be free to continue your efforts. With Dilly's help."

"Yes indeed, Your Majesty!" Nort said. He touched his chin. No beard yet, he thought as the queen produced a ring of keys and opened the door of his cell. He wouldn't need a ballad after all.

17

HO IS SHE?" THE FIRST MAN ASKED.

"A horse thief and a witch," Beaknose crowed. "Vantor will want this one."

The nearest bandits looked at Meg, surprised. Beaknose made Meg sit with the other prisoners, but he stayed nearby. Meg noticed his nose was still swollen.

The fighting died down quickly. Meg soon saw the reason as Vantor hauled the Bandit Queen into the firelight. She was bruised and limping, and there was a terrible gash across her face. "Where's the gold?" he demanded.

The woman said nothing. Her eyes flickered across the prisoners.

"Where's my treasure?" Vantor shouted.

Still the woman refused to speak.

"Search the camp," Vantor told the men nearest him.

"Your Highness, look what we found," Beaknose called, pulling Meg into the light.

Vantor dumped the Bandit Queen on the ground and stepped forward to look at Meg. He smiled slowly. Then he turned to address his men. "We have the witch!"

The Bandit Queen stared at Meg. "*She's* the witch?" At her tone, the bandits snickered, and Vantor's men peered at Meg uncertainly.

"Don't try to fool me," Vantor told the Bandit Queen. "We know you're in league with the crone." He reached out to slap Meg. "Who has disguised herself as a young girl! Show your true face, evil one!"

"*You're* evil," Meg told him.

But Vantor had turned away, raising his voice. "We have the witch! We have the bandits! We'll soon get the dragon's bones back, and then—we'll have half a kingdom!"

The men yelled.

"But not," the Bandit Queen put in, "without the missing princess."

Did it count if he had found her and didn't know it? Meg wondered.

The tall prince glared at the bandit leader. "I'll find the lost princess as easily as I found you."

Just then Vantor's men parted to make way for Bear, who came into view carrying the dragon bones on his large shoulder.

"And the gold?" Vantor asked sharply.

Bear shook his head. "Nothing."

"They've hidden it. I'll take our prisoners to the king

of Greeve. Except for the children. They stay here as hostages." Vantor gave the Bandit Queen a triumphant look. "Don't bother feeding them," he added.

Vantor's men began separating the children from the other prisoners. Meg's heart lurched as the smallest ones cried. If she were queen of Greeve—

Meg looked around, surprised by her own thoughts. How *would* she help these people? She couldn't imagine throwing them in the dungeons.

"Wait," the Bandit Queen said.

Vantor lifted a hand, and all movement stopped.

"I'll tell you where the gold is on one condition."

"What's that?"

"Let the others go. Keep me."

"That'll hardly please the king," Vantor scoffed.

"Then keep me along with my most senior men. Let the young ones go."

Vantor pursed his lips, obviously pleased by this turn of events. "All right. As soon as we have the gold, everyone under"—he looked around at the bandits—"thirteen may go free."

"And the mothers of young children," the Bandit Queen prompted.

"Agreed," Vantor said. "Where is the treasure?"

"Give me your word."

"On my oath as Prince Vantor of Rogast, I swear it."

"I'll show you," said the bandits' leader, standing with battered dignity.

✠

Dorn and Dagle were wakened from a sound sleep on their beds of rock and dirt by the bellows of the frightened cow, tethered just beyond reach of the firelight. The princes sprang up, snatching at their swords.

"Who's there?" Dorn called.

A growl answered them.

"Wolves," Dagle cried. "They're after our cow!"

Dorn and Dagle flung themselves into the darkness, swords swinging. A wolf leaped at Dorn, but he caught it with the edge of his blade. It fell back. Another launched its body at Dagle, and he fended it off. The rest of the pack closed in on the cow, which was calling helplessly.

Dorn and Dagle quickly fought their way to the sides of the terrified animal and began a spirited defense. Half a dozen wolves had fallen before the others gave up and slunk away into the night.

"Are you all right?" Dagle asked the cow, panting.

"Bring her over by the fire," Dorn said. "In case they come back."

"I'll take the first watch," Dagle told his brother.

Queen Istilda managed to get horses for Dilly and Nort. One horse, actually, since it turned out Dilly didn't know how to ride. Now she sat behind Nort, holding a lantern as they rode east arguing. It started when Nort asked if Prince Bain had returned to the castle.

"Yes."

Nort stopped the horse. "Then how are we going to find her?"

"She took the road east, right?"

Nort nodded.

"Well, something must have gone wrong. That crazy horse threw her, or she lost her way."

"With the compass?"

"Or she lost the compass, or she ran into the bandits, or she got sick."

"Or Prince Bain caught her," Nort said, twitching the horse's reins.

"In which case, we'll rescue her."

"But what if he—"

"He's not the type," Dilly announced firmly. "I can see him taking her shoes away and making her walk clear to Crown. That'd be his idea of a good joke."

"I hope you're right." Nort urged the horse forward again. "I still don't understand why you had to tell the queen anything."

"Because," Dilly snapped, "she promised she would leave us alone as long as nothing went wrong. And now something has."

Nort didn't bother to answer.

"You would still be in the dungeons if I hadn't told," Dilly told him.

"I hadn't noticed," Nort said meanly.

They rode on in an irritable silence for nearly half an hour before Nort stopped. "This is stupid, Dilly. She could be anywhere."

"We have to try," Dilly pointed out.

"I've got an idea."

"What?"

"Magic," Nort told her.

"We don't have any magic."

"But the wizard does."

"What can he do?"

"He made the spell for finding Cam. Now he can prove it worked."

"You did say he liked Meg," Dilly said.

Nort slid off the horse. "I think he'll help."

"What about me?"

"You can go to that farm and ask the witch. One way or another—"

"We're going to find Meg," Dilly concluded.

Nort convinced Dilly to take the horse, since she had farther to go. "Just hold the reins. Like that. He's a calm sort. You'll be all right." Nort turned about to retrace his steps, trying not to think about dungeons.

"Good luck!" Dilly called after him.

It was still night when Nort reached Crown. He soon discovered he didn't know where to find Lex. Nort wandered dozens of streets, searching for the wizard's house, but there was no sign of it. Nort finally admitted that it was too dark for him to recognize the place even if he passed right by it. He sank down in the nearest doorway to wait for morning.

Vantor and a group of his men left the camp with the Bandit Queen. The rest of the prisoners waited sullenly.

Meg thought she saw her scarf flit by at one point,

but maybe it was just a bat, and whatever it was, it didn't stay.

After a long while, Vantor came back with the queen. His men carried eleven great chests.

"Well?" the Bandit Queen said. "I kept my part of the bargain."

"So you did," Vantor said. He pointed to six of his men. "You'll guard my gold till we have time to move it. The rest of you—get these wretches moving."

"All of them, Your Highness?" Beaknose asked.

"All of them."

"The word of a prince means nothing!" Alya cried.

"It's my turn to laugh," Vantor said. He took his sword and lifted it near her face, only to cut off one of her black curls. "You won't need this after the king takes your pretty head."

She spat at him, but Vantor stepped back, smiling. "If you're lucky, maybe all he'll do to the brats is lock them up in the dungeons for the rest of their lives."

Dilly clopped along between the trees in the dim light of early dawn. Really, riding a horse wasn't so bad once you got used to it.

She heard the procession moving toward her long before it reached her.

Dilly hesitated for an instant, then made the horse leave the road. Behind a screen of trees, she climbed down and stood silently, holding the horse's bridle still.

Soon Prince Vantor came into view, riding yet another large steed. Behind him marched ranks of guards surrounding a ragged bunch of prisoners.

At the head of the group of captives was a black-haired woman—and Meg.

Dilly gasped. No one heard her above the tramping of so many feet.

Dilly stood watching as they all passed by. Even small children, their hands bound like the grownups'. "That Vantor," Dilly whispered, angry.

There was no point in going to the farm now. But how could she help Meg? Dilly supposed Meg might be able to talk her way out of this one, but not without a witness or two. What's more, the queen should know what was happening.

Dilly congratulated herself on having chosen the north side of the road. She led the horse deeper into the trees. If she cut through the woods, she should be able to beat Vantor to the castle.

Vantor's procession had walked a long while when Meg murmured to the Bandit Queen, "Do you still have it?"

Alya raised one bruised eyebrow wryly. "Yes."

The counterspell was in Meg's pocket, and her hands were still tied, but at least she knew Cam was close by.

"Are you the witch?" the Bandit Queen breathed.

The closest guard shoved her. "Shut up."

Meg waited a moment before shaking her head.

"He won't like being made a fool of," Alya said softly.

At another look from the guard, they trudged on without speaking.

They were nearly to the castle when Meg's scarf caught up with them. One moment Meg's neck was bare; the next it was adorned with her wandering friend. The Bandit Queen looked over inquiringly, but said nothing.

Meg tried to whisper a few suggestions to the scarf, hoping it would free her, but the thing seemed unconvinced her situation was dire. It simply lolled across her shoulders as she tramped up the hill to her home.

The tower was still invisible, she noticed in the pink light of dawn.

Nort must have dozed off, because the next thing he knew he was being roundly cursed and thrown into the street by the owner of the front steps he'd been sitting on. Nort stumbled away, rubbing his eyes. The sun was shining, and he knew he had been right to wait. All of the buildings looked different in the morning light.

The wizard's house was in the southwest quadrant of the city, Nort decided. He forced himself to go all the way to the southern wall of Crown and begin a systematic sweep of every street lined with private homes rather than shops.

His stomach soon demanded breakfast. Fortunately, the queen had given him a small bag of coins. Nort bought a paper-wrapped omelette from a street vendor, reviving himself considerably.

He must have been down twelve streets when he passed a row of wealthy-looking homes and saw something very strange. One of the houses appeared to have vanished. Nort could see the deep hole where its cellar must have lain, the private flower garden behind it, and the trim gate leading up to it. But the house itself was gone.

Three men in servants' livery stood stiffly in front of the house, guarding its absence. Nort found himself picturing Meg dropping a little bottle into Dock's hand. Flushing with guilt, Nort hurried on.

He came across four more invisible homes in his wanderings. He was standing in front of the fourth when he heard a voice behind his shoulder. "Sad, in'it?"

He spun around. One of Dock's boys greeted him with a grin. "Very," Nort managed to say. He walked on, and the boy followed.

"Been a regular rash of invisibility in town. Startin' with Lady Darlton-Stanleyshell's fancy clothes in the middle of the market."

Nort laughed.

They walked farther. The boy, who offered his name as Jess, also described an elaborate theft involving turning a gold necklace invisible.

"Problem is, nobody wants to buy invisible gold," Jess said morosely.

Nort tried not to laugh again.

"So what are you doin'?" the boy asked. "I seen you goin' up and down awhile now."

"I'm trying to find that wizard." Nort didn't ask for help, afraid Jess would want some extravagant kind of payment.

Sure enough: "You wouldn't know where my friend could get any more of that invisibility juice, would you? Or," Jess said thoughtfully, "somethin' to make a gold necklace visible?"

"Sorry."

They passed another invisible house.

"Why did he do all this?" Nort asked.

"It's a regular lark eatin' the best invisible food an' swipin' trinkets while a bunch of rich folks run around shriekin' about the curse of Great-Aunt Lily's ghost what left them all their money," Jess observed.

"Ah."

"So why're you after the wizard now? Where's your mistress?"

Nort sighed. "I've lost her. I was hoping the wizard would help me find her."

"I might show you the wizard's house, if the price was right," Jess said.

"I don't have any magic bottles."

"Dock was real taken with that witch girl," Jess told him. "What *have* you got?"

Nort jingled the rest of his coins.

"Why din't you say so? Come on."

18

ILLY NEARLY GOT KNOCKED OFF THE HORSE by low-hanging branches more than once as she rode through the woods, but somehow she stayed on, and eventually she came trotting across the meadow to the stables. She jumped down, tossed the reins to a startled groom, and ran into the castle.

The fourth-floor housekeeper tried to stop her. "Dilly, where *have* you been?"

Dilly shook Sterga's hand off and raced up the stairs, calling back, "Queen's business!"

Finally she reached the queen's chambers and banged on the door. Then Maude wouldn't let her in. Dilly argued for ten precious minutes before she found out the queen wasn't even there.

After that Sterga *insisted* on talking with her, or rather at her, and Dilly nearly lost her position. Sterga didn't believe the queen had asked Dilly for a single thing. By the time Dilly had apologized enough to please the woman, the castle was already buzzing with the news that Vantor had won the contest. Dilly followed the others to the throne room. Hanak made the castle servants wait out in the hallway, but he left the doors open so they could hear the proceedings.

Bain's manservant was lurking outside the throne room doors, Dilly noted with distaste. When he saw her looking at him, he wandered down the hall into the king's library. "As if he would read a book," Dilly muttered.

Nort followed the boy through a maze of streets.

"This isn't the same house," Nort said at last, staring up at the six brass columns and black velvet door.

"He changes the look of it every few days," Jess explained. "We pass by here regular just to see what he's done."

Nort handed the coins over gratefully. He would never have found the house again without the boy's help.

Jess disappeared into the streets as Nort pounded on the wizard's door. "Lex! Hey, let me in! Please? It's Nort!"

The door creaked open. But no apples appeared, and Nort didn't know which way to go. The door shut behind him. "Meg's in trouble," he called. "We need your help!"

"Really? What happened?" Lex's disembodied voice asked. With a popping sound, the young wizard appeared, wearing black pajamas decorated with drops of blood that actually trickled.

"She never came back!" Nort exclaimed. "I don't know if she found Cam or not, or got lost or hurt or caught or—"

"Come along," Lex said. "You can tell me over hot chocolate."

"There's no time!"

Lex turned around. "There is always time for hot chocolate," he said severely.

Nort closed his mouth and followed the wizard.

Nort had to admit his head seemed clearer once he was sitting down sipping a great steaming mug of chocolate.

Meanwhile, Lex called his three sparks to give them instructions. Soon they were gone again.

"Now," said the wizard. "Tell me everything you know."

Nort explained about Bain and the pond—

"You had to pretend you were Dilly's boyfriend?" Lex asked with interest. "Was it fun?"

"No." Nort told Lex about Meg and the horse.

"A lively one, you say," the wizard remarked. "Go on."

"That's all," Nort said. "I went after her, but they caught me and put me in the dungeons. Then the queen let me out. Now Dilly's gone to ask the witch for help, and I—"

"You've come to me," Lex said sagely.

Nort nodded.

Meg moved along the passageways of the castle with the bandits as if in a dream. Any moment someone will recognize me, she thought. But no one did. She looked down at her hands. They were grimy and tan. Her dress was tattered and muddy and limp. She supposed her face must be just as bad.

They stopped outside the throne room, where a throng of servants watched them curiously. Meg had a single glimpse of Dilly's worried face. With a final shuffling of prisoners, Meg and the Bandit Queen were dragged into the throne room behind Vantor. Meg looked over her shoulder. The other bandits stood in a bunch at the back of the room.

The sides of the throne room were lined with weary princes, along with a contingent of Hanak's men and various nobles of the court.

"Sire," Vantor said, sweeping a low bow.

"You may approach us," King Stromgard told the prince.

Vantor's group moved forward. "Today I bring much of what you have asked for," Vantor announced, "hoping to prove myself your heir."

"Well, what have you got?" asked the king.

Vantor signaled to Bear. "First, I have slain the dragon, and I here present you with its bones." The whispering of the spectators grew louder as Vantor's men brought the gleaming bones forward and laid them on the floor before the royal thrones. The prime minister stepped closer to get a better look. He seemed daffily pleased by this turn of events.

"Very nice," King Stromgard said, leaning forward on his throne.

Meg bit her lip, forcing herself to wait for the right moment. She caught sight of Prince Bain at the front of the room and glowered, but he didn't notice.

"Second," Vantor proclaimed, "I have captured the bandits. This woman is their leader." The prince motioned to Beaknose, and the man pushed the Bandit Queen forward, shoving her to her knees in front of the king and queen. "There you see the rest of her band," Vantor added, indicating the huddle of prisoners behind him.

"Even children?" Queen Istilda murmured.

"And this," Vantor proclaimed, "is the witch." He grabbed Meg by the arm, pulling her to stand beside him.

"She's rather young," the king observed. But his wife was gaping at Meg, her eyes wide.

"Dear," she said faintly, "that's our daughter."

The king leaned forward on his throne. *"Margaret?"*

"Yes, Father?" Meg replied.

Vantor dropped his hand from Meg's arm and turned to look at her, utterly astonished. He frantically faced the royal thrones, where he was assailed by Queen Istilda's coldest expression. Prince Bain grinned nearby. He caught Meg's eye and winked. Beside Meg, the Bandit Queen snickered. "Well done," Alya whispered.

"Majesties," Vantor sputtered, "the girl didn't—" He recovered. "What I meant to say, of course, is that I have rescued your daughter, who, far from being a witch, has obviously *been* bewitched."

"Margaret?" the king said again. "What has happened?"

Meg opened her mouth to explain, but Vantor spoke before she could begin. "Furthermore, since I found the princess in the clutches of the bandits, it is clear they've been working with the witch to foil you."

"Foil me?" the king asked. "How do you mean, young man?"

Vantor waved his hand. "To ruin your wondrous competition, of course."

Prince Bain stepped forward. "Your Majesty, if I may make a statement . . ."

"You may."

"While I have the greatest respect for Prince Vantor, I must question the condition of these bones, which appear to have suffered the ravages of time, being much more dry and polished than one would expect from a recent kill."

Vantor's face darkened. "*You* bring nothing to this room but false accusations! Has churlish envy stolen your manners?"

Bain went on as if Vantor had not spoken. "And

those peasants—they seem like humble folk to me. How do we know they are truly bandits?"

"Because *this* one—" Vantor began, pointing at the Bandit Queen. He caught himself.

"Yes?" Bain asked silkily.

"This one robbed me on the mountainside three days ago," Vantor hissed.

King Stromgard laughed. "And now you have turned the tables. No need to be ashamed, lad. The whole castle's been talking about your unfortunate encounter."

"There's even a lute ballad," the prime minister piped up, but he quieted again at a look from the king.

"What did she steal?" Bain asked.

Vantor flushed. "My horse," he said. "And a sword my father gave me."

"That's not all!" Meg cried, unable to restrain herself any longer. "You stole all of the dragon's gold, and then the bandits stole it from you, and then you stole it back!"

The king frowned. "Now, Margaret, you mustn't go telling tales on this heroic young man. He did just rescue you."

Meg's jaw dropped. "He did not! He thought I was a bandit, and a witch, and a horse thief!"

"Horse thief?" the queen asked.

"I suspect the princess can shed a great deal of light on my fellow contestant's claims," Bain said.

"Your Majesties," Vantor inserted quickly, "I confess the young lady's condition puzzled me, but I didn't wish to upset her delicate mental state."

"Delicate *what*?" Meg repeated, outraged.

"Here," Vantor continued in his rich voice, "is your daughter, delivered safely into your arms. Here are the bandits, and the dragon's bones, and"—he shot Bain an awful look—"the treasure."

From the back of the room, four of Vantor's men triumphantly produced a carved wooden chest. They carried it forward and opened it before the monarchs, displaying jewels and coins and goblets. Everyone in the room craned their necks to see. The king brightened.

Vantor seized the moment. "I will shortly pursue the witch, particularly in the hope that she may restore the princess to her usual gracious and regal self." Vantor took Meg's arm again. The gesture may have appeared fond this time, but the prince's fingers pressed tightly, silently threatening.

The king nodded. "Well, everything does seem to be in order."

"One chest?" Bain asked, taking another step forward. "I confess I cannot believe a dragon that size (however long dead and desiccated) could manage to collect only a single chest of treasure during its two hundred or more years of existence."

The king tilted his head, considering. "It is a bit odd."

"Treasure's treasure," the prime minister said, ogling the gold.

But Vantor had put his hand on his sword hilt and

stepped toward Bain. "Foul prince! I'll meet you on the dueling field to defend my honor!"

Bain drew his sword. "Who needs a field?" he said easily.

"Oooh," some thirty ladies of the court gasped at once.

Vantor leaped at Bain, slashing hard, but Bain parried and slipped aside. Vantor followed him through the room, and they dueled madly. The crowd drew back.

"Here now," said King Stromgard. "Stop that at once!"

Vantor was beyond listening, charging after Bain with a vengeance. Bain defended himself elegantly, even drawing a dagger in his other hand to defend his left flank. The two princes danced right around the prisoners. Bain almost lost his balance, dropping the dagger near Alya's feet. He spun free of Meg and her companion, attacking Vantor with a flurry of thrusts that drove the prince toward the back of the room. The guards were as riveted by the fight as everyone else.

Only Meg saw the Bandit Queen crouch quickly to retrieve the fallen dagger. Only Meg saw Alya cut her hands free of the bonds that held her. As the fight circled through the room, the crowd shifted around Meg and the Bandit Queen. With a quick smile, Alya slipped a silver chain from her neck and dropped it over Meg's head.

Meg didn't have time to say thank you, watching the bandit slither between brocade-clad courtiers. A scuffle broke out near the door. It took a few moments for the court to notice that another fight had begun, this one among the prisoners.

Vantor, who was rapidly losing ground, glanced back. "Bain," he said, panting. "The bandits are getting loose."

Bain looked up. "Are they?" He reached out to the nobleman nearest him to relieve him of his sword. "Very good." Bain threw the second sword in a high arc across the room. Even people well out of range of the blade ducked. "Sister!" Bain called, and a slim hand reached out of the fray to catch the hilt.

Then Bain himself slipped into the panicking crowd.

"Bain!" Vantor roared, diving after him.

Hanak's men finally moved. The nearest princes caught on and rushed to join them. A few of the noblemen followed suit, while the rest of the courtiers tried their best to stay out of the way.

"Did you see that, dear?" Queen Istilda remarked.

The king had stood up and was trying to look through the crowd. "Not precisely."

"One of those princes appears to be a bandit."

Meg smiled. It was harder to dislike Bain now that she knew he had tricked her father. Now that she had Cam back.

"What? Who?" said the king.

"Prince Bain," the queen told him. "He's a bandit."

With a final wild tangle, the throne room was clear. Feet pounded away outside. The last of Vantor's men surged into the passageway, and the courtiers fled. The prime minister excused himself hastily. Hanak's guards were already gone, leaving only a single man behind to watch the royal family.

Meg's father turned his attention to her. "Margaret, go to your room."

"Not until you listen," she said. "Vantor is a liar and a thief!"

"*Bain* is a liar and a thief," the king told her. "I just found out. Guard, escort my daughter to her room."

"So you can marry me to Prince Vantor?" Meg demanded. "This morning I watched him steal a mountain of dragon's gold, break his sworn word, and threaten small children. He's not worthy to be king of·Greeve or anyplace else!"

"I never thought," His Majesty said heavily, "that you would take your dislike of your duties to the extent of besmirching a young man's character. Guard!"

The remaining guard stepped to Meg's side. He paused, reluctant.

"I won't go bound in my own home," the princess told him, holding out her hands. The guard drew his knife and carefully cut the ropes away.

"Thank you." Meg reached awkwardly into her hidden pocket to take out a little wooden box. She twisted it, then touched it to the silver box dangling around her neck. There was a blast of light and wind—and Cam was suddenly sprawled on the floor at Meg's feet.

"Get up," she told him.

The king and queen watched, speechless, as Cam

scrambled to his feet. Meg tugged the gardener's boy after her, charging out onto the royal balcony. "I've got magic," she said breathlessly.

Cam nodded once. Meg looked down at the ground far below, grasped the scarf with her free hand, and yelled, "Float!" Then she and Cam jumped.

19

HE BANDITS RAN THROUGH THE HALLS OF the castle with Hanak's guards, a handful of princes, and Vantor's men on their heels. It didn't help the bandits that they had to carry the smallest children. On the other hand, all of the castle servants had gathered just outside the throne room to listen to Vantor's news. Hanak's men were forced to lower their swords and weave through a mass of screaming chambermaids to get at their quarry.

Hanak caught one little bandit boy by the arm, but the child wriggled loose and disappeared again.

Vantor nearly gutted the head housekeeper and had to stop and apologize before the other servants would let him by, only to find that the Bandit Queen and five of her men had managed to barricade the hallway almost instantaneously with heavy furniture from the king's library. Bain's manservant was there with them, grinning at the prince's rage and wielding a mean broadsword.

Vantor and his men fought hard, but the place was a bot-
tleneck and the bandits were seasoned fighters.

On the other side of the barricade, the rest of Vantor's former prisoners raced down the great steps and
across the courtyard. "To the stables!" Bain yelled.

A moment later, his sword tip was at the throat of
the stable master. "Which one is Vantor's horse?" The
frightened man gestured to a groom to fetch the prince's
newest mount. Meanwhile, the other bandits invaded
the stables and began bringing out horses as fast as they
could.

Alya eventually abandoned her blockade and hurtled
away down the halls, with Vantor and Hanak right behind her. She charged through the castle gate just as the
other bandits burst across the stable yard on horseback.
Bain brought up the rear on Vantor's latest stallion. As
the last of the bandits leaped onto the waiting horses,
Bain pulled his sister up behind him. He waved cheerily
to his pursuers as he galloped off.

Vantor and Hanak and their men poured after the
bandits, but they were soon outdistanced. Vantor
stormed into the stable yard, pulling the stable master to
his feet. "Get me another horse!"

"But, sir—"

"This terrible country *owes* me a horse!" Vantor
howled.

"But, sir—all that's left is a mule!"

Vantor spun about. "No matter. I know where they're
headed." He started to marshal his men.

"Where are they going?" Hanak asked, stepping up behind him.

Vantor didn't answer for a moment. Then he said begrudgingly, "East."

"For now. But what's to stop them from leaving the road around the first bend?"

Vantor shrugged with ill-concealed temper. "You're right, of course."

Hanak was watching him closely. "They would hardly go back to their previous camp."

"No," Vantor replied. He took a deep breath, thinking. "We should split up, to cover more ground."

"Of course." Hanak paused. "You've been hunting these robbers for days. Where do you suggest we begin?"

Vantor smiled grimly. "My men and I will march toward the moors, where they have often hidden. And you—if they do leave the road, they'll vanish into those woods."

Hanak nodded. "We set out together and watch for any sign of them leaving the road."

The last of the princes strolled disconsolately through the half-empty camp. "No point in sticking around if Vantor's won," said a thin prince whose arms were covered in ceremonial tattoos.

"He lost those bandits," said another.

"For the moment," chimed in a muscle-bound type. The rest soon took up the chorus.

"Did you see the princess?"

"Mm-hmm. The daring ragamuffin type."

"Freckled, even."

"Not what I expected."

The princes stared at each other. A pudgy blond said, "I heard the king of Weir's daughter has been kidnapped by an evil sorcerer."

"Really? That's east of here."

The blond prince nodded.

"They say she looks like a spring morning," said the tattooed prince.

"How, exactly?" the muscular prince asked.

"Cheeks like apple blossoms, lips like an April sunrise, eyes like twin drops of rain, I believe it was."

"What are we waiting for?" said one of the others.

Soon the colorful tents were being folded up.

Meg and Cam plummeted for a terrifying second. Then the scarf flipped its tail, and they floated jerkily. Meg was just feeling relieved when the scarf decided to have some fun. It bounced them and rolled them. Suddenly Meg and Cam soared up over the meadow to an alarming height.

"Meg!" Cam cried.

"The woods," Meg called to the scarf. "We want to go to the woods!"

The scarf slowed them again, and they drifted lazily toward the ground.

"I hope we don't hit the tower," said Meg.

"What tower?" Cam asked, looking sideways over the empty meadow.

Some of the servants were running toward them from the castle. Meg and Cam twirled, suspended in midair at about the height of a young tree.

"Don't let us get caught!" Meg barked. The scarf ignored her. "Please?" she added.

The servants reached them and began jumping, trying to catch Meg and Cam's dangling feet.

All of a sudden Meg and Cam felt themselves zoom back up and over the trees at the edge of the woods, leaving the castle far behind.

"Floating frogs," Meg said, feeling a little green. A bird swerved to avoid them.

"Meg," Cam asked. "*What* is going on?"

As the prince and the guard captain parted to organize their forces, they heard yelling from the courtyard.

"Now what?" Hanak barked, striding back toward the castle.

One of the servants skidded to a stop in front of him. "It's the princess. She's gone again."

"How is that possible?"

Vantor joined Hanak. "What happened?"

"Princess Margaret leaped off the balcony with some kind of magic and floated away over the woods!"

"Why would she do such a thing?" Vantor asked impatiently.

The servant said nothing.

"Well?"

"It appears she isn't eager to have you as her groom," Hanak remarked to the prince. He called four of his men. "Search the woods for the princess. Bring her home as quickly and gently as you can."

Vantor's face darkened. He turned away to shout at his own men.

Moments later, Prince Vantor's forces were marching east, with Hanak's men bringing up the rear.

They were well on their way when Vantor sent Beaknose sneaking ahead to crush the underbrush to one side of the road, making it look as if the bandits had passed into the woods. Soon after, he called a halt and walked back to speak to Hanak.

"It's not enough to be certain, but they might have left the road," he told the guard captain. Vantor led Hanak over to see.

Hanak examined the spot. "Very well," he said. "We'll part company here." He led his men into the woods as Vantor's forces traveled on.

Once Hanak's men were well within the trees, he gathered them together. "I don't trust that Vantor," he said bluntly. Hanak indicated two of the guards. "You and Pagget are going to track the prince and his men from close at hand. Don't let them see you. The rest of us will follow at a distance. If anything happens, come back and tell us."

"Do you think the princess is right?" one man asked. "About the prince being a bad lot?"

"I do," he said. "And we're going to find out exactly what his game is." He looked around at his guardsmen. "Unless you fancy having him for a king."

"I'd rather swallow a rotted rodent," someone called. The others murmured their agreement.

"I thought not," said Hanak.

"And the bandits?" old Arbel asked.

"Vantor's going to lead us straight to them," the guard captain said.

Meg and Cam were long gone, but King Stromgard still stood on the balcony with his mouth open.

Queen Istilda came up beside him. "Are you happy now?"

"How can you say such a thing?" the king bellowed. "I arrange a glorious quest, a marriage any princess would envy, and that ungrateful child *defies* me!"

The servants coming back across the meadow averted their eyes from the sight of the enraged king.

"Dear," the queen said, pulling his arm, "I want to show you something." The king allowed her to lead him into the empty throne room. The dragon bones still lay on the floor. Beside them, the contents of treasure chest had been turned out in a pile.

"Who did that?" the king asked.

"I did," his wife said.

"What for?"

"I was looking for something."

"What could you possibly be looking for?"

The queen crouched to run her hands through the scattering of golden trinkets and gemstones. "My aunt Mariana was wearing her grandmother's jewels when that creature took her."

The king squatted beside his wife to examine the treasure.

"They're not here," the queen said. "A gold bracelet studded with sapphires and a string of emeralds twined about with pearls. My mother told me the tale more than once, with a great many details and rather too much relish."

"Surely—" the king said, and stopped.

"Perhaps your thief is no liar. Perhaps your hero is a thief," Queen Istilda told him.

"Nonsense!" the king said. But he didn't sound quite so certain.

"One chest?" the queen reminded him.

At second glance, the gems in the heap *were* rather second-rate. Nearly half the coins were silver. "It's not much of a hoard," King Stromgard admitted. He reached over to touch the dragon's bones. "They aren't fresh at all." He stood. "Margaret—"

"Was right," the queen said, standing to face him. She paused delicately. "How would you feel if your father took the word of a stranger over yours?"

"She's behaved badly," the king muttered.

"So have you," his wife said.

"Hmmph." The king was silent for a moment. Then he rallied. "How could Margaret know anything about all this?"

"Because," the queen said, "she and her friends have been sneaking about interfering with your contest for days."

"She was in the tower—" the king began, but he interrupted himself. "She wasn't, was she?"

"Not for long."

King Stromgard narrowed his eyes. "You knew," he grumbled.

"I found out two days ago."

"Why didn't you inform me?" he asked, but the bluster was gone from his voice.

The queen smiled. "I thought she was doing rather a good job."

"I—I suppose I ought to tell her she needn't marry that Vantor fellow." The king plumped down on his throne, resting his bearded chin in his hands. "But she's gone off again."

"I have an idea how we can find her," the queen said thoughtfully.

Lex listened to voices Nort couldn't hear as the sparks scribbled the air. "Well," the boy wizard said at last, "that's quite a story!"

"What? What did they say?"

"It seems the tall prince brought Meg to the castle

with some bandits, then everyone started fighting and running around, and Meg jumped off the balcony."

Nort nearly dropped his mug. "Is she all right?"

"Oh yes. She flew away with a boy."

"Cam!" Nort said. "The counterspell worked!"

"Of course it did." Lex tapped his round fingers on the table. "Where will she go now?"

"Maybe the farm. Cam's sister's there. And the witch."

"That's not good," Lex said. "The king and queen just rode out the gates to find her. Actually, the king and some of his noblemen were walking. The queen was riding a mule."

"They won't know where she is."

"Maybe they will. Your friend Dilly is with them."

"Oh!" Nort said. "We've got to warn Meg!"

Lex stood up. "I have a lot of work to do," he said doubtfully. He ruffled a stack of parchment pages.

"You're really going to stay here?" Nort asked, astonished.

"I should," Lex said. The young wizard paused, looking expectantly at Nort.

Nort took his cue. "We need your help."

"Really?"

"Really truly."

Lex grinned. "You've convinced me! Let's go!"

"Um, Lex."

"What?"

"Maybe you could change your clothes first," Nort suggested.

Lex remembered his bleeding pajamas. "Oh. Right." He snapped his fingers. In an instant, he was wearing a dramatic black cloak and a curlicued gold mask.

"A mask?" Nort said.

"My true identity must not be known," Lex announced grandly.

"If I were a wizard, I'd use magic to disguise myself as someone else."

"Oh, very good!" Lex snapped his fingers once more. With a squiggle of light, he turned into an ogre, a blue one with long red fangs. Lex spun around, showing off his new look. "Do you want me to change you, too?" he inquired in a voice like iron walls falling onto rocks.

"No, thanks." Nort backed away. "You need something less noticeable, actually."

Lex dropped his heavy claws. "You don't like it?"

Nort shook his head.

The ogre snapped his fingers with some difficulty. Lex reappeared, looking like himself again. Now he was dressed in a tan shirt with black breeches and boots. The only oddity was his cap, which, though brown, was topped with what appeared to be a burning phoenix feather. Nort gestured at the feather.

"You're no fun," Lex complained. The feather vanished. Lex went to the door. "Coming?"

"Can't you zap us there?" Nort asked.

"Nope. Only inside the house."

Nort followed him. "So you have a magic carriage out back, right?"

"I had a magic carpet," Lex said, "but I traded it for something better."

"What's that?" Nort asked.

"Peanut butter."

"Peanut butter?"

"A lot of it," Lex said. "Best quality. I'll make you a sandwich when we get back."

20

ORN AND DAGLE STOOD LOOKING AT THEIR
trap with unabashed awe. The trunks of young
trees rose like dragon's wings into the morning,
perfectly poised to spring back and slam their glittering
prey into the deep pit.

"It's beautiful," Dagle breathed.

Dorn wiped his eye on his sleeve. "Yes, it is."

"Aren't we going to put the cow in?" Dagle asked.

"Oh. Right. The bait."

The princes turned around.

The cow was gone.

"No!" Dorn cried.

"It wasn't wolves, was it?" Dagle said, puzzled.

Dorn examined the ground where the cow had been
tethered. "There's no blood."

"Then what happened?"

Dorn picked up the frayed end of the rope that had

held the cow in their camp. "Looks like she worried at her tether for so long that she pulled free."

"We'll have to get another cow. Unless we can find her."

"First let's go back to the castle and find ourselves a well-cooked meal," Dorn said.

"Bacon and eggs!" Dagle exclaimed, considerably cheered.

It may be easy to attack a bandit camp in the dead of night when the bandits are not expecting you. It is more difficult to guard a camp against bandits who know its every twig and pebble, especially when you are not expecting them. Or so Vantor's guards discovered. They fought as best they could, but the Bandit Queen was soon in possession of her camp again. "Pack up!" Alya yelled.

The bandit tribe scrambled to take everything that hadn't been destroyed by Vantor's men. Including the gold.

"Be grateful my quarrel is with your leader," the Bandit Queen told Vantor's guards. She flipped the nose of the nearest. "We've done this to you twice now. Perhaps you should rethink your loyalties."

The bandits rode out.

When Vantor arrived some time later, he saw nothing but six battle-bruised men tied to trees.

"We found the bandits once, we'll find them again," the prince announced. "Now move out!"

"Your Highness . . ." asked one of the men riding with him.

"What?"

"Aren't we going to untie them?"

"They can rot here. May their last thought be regret for losing my treasure." Prince Vantor spat on the ground and strode off. The rest of the men followed him uneasily.

Behind the trees, Hanak's spies slipped away to find their captain.

An army marched down the Dragon Crags into Greeve. Two armies, actually—a large force from Tarylon and another from Lors. When they came within sight of the castle, the marchers paused.

King Tark brought his horse up alongside King Jal's. "We capture Greeve's royal seat—"

"And Greeve is ours. Stromgard will have no choice."

"It's a nice little kingdom," Tark said with a sideways look. "Reparation for our pain and trouble?"

"We split the place right down the middle," said Jal. "West for you, east for me."

"Only proper," Tark agreed, pleased. "You don't mind about the castle and the city?"

Jal shook his head. "Lot of upkeep, that. We both want what's just south of us, I'd say."

"Once we get our sons back," Tark reminded the other monarch.

Jal grimaced. "After that."

At a sign from the two kings, the army rode down the royal road to surround the castle. Stromgard would have been outraged if he had been at home to see.

On the other side of the kingdom, Bain and his sister surveyed their new camp. Old camp, really, a site at the foot of the mountains they sometimes used when the king's guards sniffed about the other camp too closely. The tents were up. The sentries were posted. The wounded had been tended. Children were laughing again. In the middle of it all sat eleven chests filled with dragon gold.

"So it's over," the Bandit Queen said, polishing her dagger absently on the hem of her tunic. She sat with her brother on the hill overlooking the camp.

"Alya, what do you intend to do now?"

She looked at him, surprised. "We'll move on. We've got enough to make a good life to the south."

"And the dragon won't complain," Bain said thoughtfully. "She's a pile of bones."

"But?" Alya stopped polishing the dagger.

"But nothing."

The Bandit Queen narrowed her eyes. "You can't fool me. You're put out over losing to that Vantor."

"He didn't win!"

"Then who did?"

Bain smiled slowly. "Why, the princess."

"I liked her," Alya admitted.

Bain began whistling under his breath.

"Are you worried?" his sister asked him.

"The prince of Rogast is capable of anything."

"Besides," Alya said sweetly, "you want to see how the story ends."

"Yes. I do." Bain was already in motion and raising his voice. "Feg!"

It wasn't long before the scarf tired of Meg and Cam's adventure and dropped them in the middle of the Witch's Wood.

"I'm beginning to recognize every root in this place," Meg said, resigned. She tromped off in the direction of Janna's farm.

"Tell me the rest," Cam said, following her. "I kept missing bits while we were flying."

"First tell me what it was like inside that spell."

Cam hesitated. Finally he said, "Like walking around in the fog, lost. When you know who you are, but not where you are."

"I'm sorry, Cam," Meg said miserably.

"It's not your fault. Really, Meg. Now finish your story. You couldn't find the wizard, and some street boys surrounded you?"

Meg took a deep breath and let it out again. "All right. So Dock, the leader, agreed to take us right to the wizard's door. We gave him the invisibility bottle to pay him."

"What did he do with it?"

Meg laughed. "I've been trying not to think about it."

The rest of her story took them almost to the edge of the wood. As the trees grew sparse, Cam caught Meg's arm. "What are you going to do now?"

She faced him. "What I've always wanted. I'm leaving this stupid kingdom to make my fortune, like a prince in one of the tales."

"They're not true, you know," Cam said quietly.

Meg stared at him for a long, grim moment. "Yes they are," she hissed. The scarf came down and perched on top of her head. All of its eyes glared at Cam, as if to punctuate Meg's remarks.

Cam spoke into the sudden silence. "Look, Meg. I'm not saying princes don't have adventures. But I'll bet a lot of them get eaten by the first dragon they come to."

Meg grinned suddenly. "I have my own dragon." Then she grew serious. "Aren't you coming with me?"

Cam dropped his head, scuffing the dead leaves and dirt with his toe. "I'm not saying I won't. It's just that— the whole time I was locked up in that spell, I missed you, I missed my sister, I missed my breakfast. But mostly I missed my garden."

Meg didn't know what to say.

"You want all this magic," Cam said, trying to explain. "But I've got magic, too."

"What?"

Cam waved his hands. "I plant seeds in the earth and they *grow*. I make them strong and good by *my* arts!"

Meg's face softened. "That is a kind of magic, I suppose."

Cam gave her a friendly push on the shoulder. "Let's have some of Janna's biscuits and talk about this later."

"All right," Meg said, pushing him back.

The air between them had lightened. Even so, they traveled the rest of the way to the farm without talking, absorbed in their separate thoughts.

Nort and Lex neared the city's north gates.

"You could call a griffin," Nort suggested.

"The talons would cut you right open."

"I meant we could ride on its back."

Lex kept going. "They're simply not designed for that."

Ahead of them, a crowd was gathering, shouting and running. Something was always happening in the city, Nort thought. "How about a cloud? You could get one to carry us."

"They're made of air and water," Lex pointed out. "We'd fall right through."

"What about—what's going on?"

This crowd wasn't the usual. Everyone Nort and Lex passed looked terrified. Ahead of them, the gates of Crown were slowly swinging shut.

Nort snatched at a man's sleeve. "What's wrong?"

"We're under attack!" the man cried as he dashed away.

Nort and Lex hurried, but they were too late. The

gates closed. The sentries lowered the heavy bars to lock them.

"Now what?" Nort asked the wizard.

Lex's mouth twisted as he thought. The crowd swirled around them, almost knocking them down more than once. Suddenly the streets were empty except for the two of them.

"I wish we had Meg's scarf," Nort said. "She told me it could float things."

"There are other ways to float. What was the tenth thing you suggested just now?" Lex asked.

"Um, magic horses?"

"That's it!" Lex looked about. "We need a horse."

All of the stables were locked tight, but Nort found a goat tethered behind a grimy house, and Lex said it would do. Nort had his doubts. When they pounded on the door, nobody would open it, so Lex magicked a silver coin into the house. Somebody within yelped gleefully and then was silent again.

Next the two boys hauled the goat around until they found a section of the city wall facing an alley. Nort had to hold the goat still while Lex set about enchanting it. The goat bleated pathetically.

"Climb on," Lex said at last.

"On there?"

"We'll both fit," Lex assured him.

Somehow they did, though the poor goat bleated the more.

"Up, goat!" Lex called. The goat made an odd noise and jumped—only to rise slowly toward the top of the wall.

Farther down the wall, one of the sentries caught sight of them and came running, lifting his crossbow.

"Move, goat!" Nort yelped.

They were over the top and starting downward when the sentry reached them. Lex flicked his fingers, and the crossbow turned into a stalk of celery.

"It's always food spells with you," Nort said breathlessly as they climbed off the goat and ran. The goat ran, too, but not in the same direction.

Nort and Lex had gone only a little way when they caught sight of the invaders. A vast army spread itself around the castle of Greeve, the last of the soldiers tramping into place as the two boys watched.

"Lex?" Nort asked.

"Right," Lex said, and called his sparks.

Earlier that morning, Dorn and Dagle had wandered around the castle for a long while, trying to find someone to give them a hot breakfast. Very few servants were about, and the ones the twins passed rushed by, unwilling to talk to them.

"We'll just have to fend for ourselves," Dorn told his brother.

Dagle followed Dorn down steps and along passageways, sniffing the air for some sign of food.

The kitchens, when they reached them, were deserted. The brothers scrounged around, happily settling for leftover chicken and mashed potatoes when they couldn't find the eggs. They were starting their second helpings when they heard the commotion. "Here now, what's this?" Dorn asked a scullery maid who had made the mistake of appearing in the pantry.

She merely shrieked and scuttled away.

"Come, brother," Dagle said.

The two emerged into the courtyard. Ahead of them, the chief housekeeper stood at the locked gate, a meager huddle of manservants around her. Dorn and Dagle approached.

"I told you, he's not at home!" the woman said shrilly.

"Open the gates," a harsh man's voice said.

The housekeeper shook her head. "You may wait on the lawns. I'm not to open the doors when my master's away."

"Give us the princes of Tarylon and Lors," another voice said.

Dorn and Dagle came up beside the housekeeper. "Those two are frogs just now," Dagle said, waving a drumstick. "Not available for conversation."

A great uproar outside the gate greeted these words. Dorn and Dagle looked at each other, surprised. " 'S true," Dorn said with a shrug.

The housekeeper turned her fierce eyes on them. "What do you mean causing trouble?"

"Trouble?" Dorn stepped to the gate. "Hey there, who are you fellows?"

A trumpet blared, and someone announced grandly, "The kings of Tarylon and Lors seek redress for the abduction and foul enchantment of their sons."

"Oh," Dagle said, catching on. "Angry parents."

21

ANTOR AND HIS MEN CAME SWEEPING DOWN
the road. Beaknose had pointed out they would
never find the bandits without horses. Vantor
had begrudgingly agreed. They would go back to the castle. Vantor's men would re-outfit in Crown while the
prince pressed the king to call him the contest winner.

"We'd better find that crazy princess," Vantor added.

Beaknose said nothing, but he touched his nose gingerly.

"Take Wott and search for her."

"Someone's coming," Beaknose said, grateful to
change the subject.

Vantor called a halt. He and his men watched the
king and queen of Greeve come over the crest of the
road, followed by the prime minister and a gaggle of
footsore noblemen. All of them were walking except the
queen, who rode a mule. "Greetings, Your Majesty,"
Vantor said.

The king frowned. "Any sign of the bandits?"

"Not yet. That is, we returned to their camp, but it was abandoned."

"Where's Hanak?"

"There were two trails. Hanak and his men followed the other, into the woods."

"I see." The king's face was glacial. Vantor looked at the queen. Her expression was just as stiff. Even the courtiers and the little servant girl seemed hostile. The prime minister stared at the ground.

"Is something wrong, Majesties?" Vantor asked.

"Oh, not at all," Stromgard said. "My daughter is missing again, the bandits have escaped, the witch is still at large, and you appear to be a liar and a thief."

Vantor's hand went to his sword hilt. "What do you mean?" he asked tightly.

"Much as I dislike that bandit prince, my wife has informed me the treasure you gave us is missing certain identifiable items, and the dragon bones are arguably in a state of advanced decay."

Vantor's face grew still. "You believe this foolishness?"

The king nodded. "I'm going to fetch my daughter home and apologize for doubting her word."

"And me?"

"I'm afraid you're disqualified," the king said. "The question remains: where is the rest of the dragon's hoard?"

Vantor smiled. "You're not going to declare me the winner?"

"Certainly not."

"Then I declare myself the winner," Vantor said softly. "And the king of Greeve." He signaled his men. They moved forward to surround the king's party.

But the queen was too quick for them. She kicked the mule, hard. The creature brayed and ran back up the road toward the castle.

"Go after her!" Vantor barked at Bear and Beaknose. The two men raced away. "Now let us proceed to retrieve my own willful queen," Vantor told his prisoners.

"Not my Margaret!" the king cried. Just behind him, Dilly turned white.

"Gag him," Vantor ordered. "And anyone else who dares to speak against me," he said as the prime minister opened his mouth. Garald snapped his mouth shut. As soon as the king's mouth was covered, Vantor sneered, "The girl is *my* Margaret now. Along with the spoils of this contest." The prince spoke in a mocking whisper. "Sadly, I suspect that bandits will get to poor old Stromgard in short order."

Hanak and his men surged through the trees into the bandits' former camp, only to find Vantor gone. "Untie them," Hanak said, gesturing toward Vantor's unfortunate guards. The men were soon brought before the captain.

"Well?" Hanak asked.

Five of Vantor's men refused to meet Hanak's eyes,

but the sixth looked up. "I'll help you! It's not like he was ever going to give us any of that gold."

The other prisoners appeared even more disheartened. Hanak noticed they didn't disagree.

"Tell me what happened," Hanak said. "No, wait. Arbel!"

"Yes, Captain."

"These men have been through a lot. Bring them water and something to eat."

"Yes, Captain."

"Sit down," Hanak said, sitting on a large rock himself. "And tell me all about it."

When Vantor's man was finished, Hanak stood. "Where do you think Vantor will go?"

The man shrugged. "He'll search the moors for those bandits. He'll want the treasure back."

"Very well." Hanak divided his guards into three groups. "You men will help me scour the moors for Vantor and the escaped bandits," he said, pointing to the largest group. He turned to the next contingent. "Arbel, you'll march to the castle with the prisoners and notify the king of what has happened."

"And us?" asked a man in the third and smallest group.

"You're going to assist the men I sent to find the princess. Pagget's in charge."

Soon Hanak and his guardsmen had dispersed to carry out their respective duties, and the bandit's camp lay empty, waiting to be reclaimed by the moors.

At Hookhorn Farm, Janna hugged Cam while Meg hugged the dragon, and after that Janna hugged Meg while Cam didn't hug Gorba.

"The magic worked!" Janna cried. "You got him back!"

"Of course it did," Gorba said with satisfaction.

Meg hugged Gorba, too. "That invisibility spell worked a little too well."

"What do you mean?"

Janna hurried to serve them shepherd's pie and milk. Then Meg had to tell the whole story over again between bites. The dragon, who had grown quite plump, draped himself over her feet as she talked.

"By my cows and hens," Janna exclaimed when Meg had finished. "What hasn't happened to you two!"

A muffled croak punctuated her words. "What was that?" Cam asked.

Janna blushed. "Just a few frogs." She busied herself taking a fresh batch of biscuits out of the oven.

Meg raised her brows. "You let them in?" A row of milk pails lined the far wall. Green heads rose to peep out at the new arrivals. Meg waved at the frog princes. One by one the heads dropped back into the buckets.

"Gorba's been a great help," Janna said defensively.

Gorba's face was smug.

The scarf chose that moment to wind itself out of Meg's pocket. "Oh!" Meg said, remembering. "I suppose I'd better give your scarf back." The scarf flipped behind her shoulder and peeked over at Gorba, looking a bit like the frogs peering over the rims of their pails.

"It's quite taken with you, lass. You'd better keep it."

"Thank you, Gorba!"

"Creature never did half that stuff for me," Gorba grumbled. "I should probably be getting home." She turned her gaze on Meg and Cam. "Now that you've found your true love and all."

Meg turned red, remembering the witch's flowery words about her friendship with the gardener's boy. Cam was no help. He chuckled. Even Janna smiled.

Meg ignored all of this as best she could. "The contest isn't over," she told the witch. "Vantor says he's won, but he's still trying to find you. And me, too, I suppose."

"He won't come *here*," Janna said comfortably. "Have a biscuit."

Nort and Lex took up their post behind a flowering bush that stood near the road leading from Crown to the castle. The wizard's sparks were full of news. "It's two kings from the north," Lex told Nort. "They're angry because their sons have been turned into frogs."

"So they just want their sons back?"

Lex shook his head. "Apparently they figure they'll take over Greeve as long as they're here."

"But the king's gone," Nort said. "Where's Hanak?"

"He and Vantor went after the bandits."

"Then there's no one left to guard the castle!" Nort said. He threw his shoulders back. "Except us."

"Still the guardsman?" Lex asked.

"*Someone* needs to take care of things," Nort said hotly.

Lex shrugged. "One king is as good as another, I would think."

"Don't you know anything?"

"Not about kings," Lex admitted without rancor.

"It's Meg's father," Nort pointed out.

"I thought she was mad at him."

"That doesn't mean she would like this. Are you going to help?"

"It might be fun," the young wizard said. "I've never stopped an army before."

"Can you?" Nort asked.

Lex frowned. "Long enough to get us into the castle."

"And destroy the invaders?"

"You mean kill them?" Lex asked. "All those men?"

"Well, no. I guess not."

"I told you, I'm not an evil wizard," Lex said reprovingly. "You can guard the castle once we're inside."

"Right," Nort said with just a touch of regret.

"Now, I can protect you magically, but I can't protect myself."

"From what?"

"From the effects of the spell. As soon as I laugh or even smile, it will stop working."

"What do you mean?" Nort asked, but Lex was already touching Nort's eyes and ears, chanting. Nort forced himself to hold still. "Get ready," Lex said. "When I tell you, you have to cover my ears. I'll cover my own eyes."

"But you won't be able to see where you're going," Nort objected.

"You'll be my guide."

They crossed the road and headed toward the army. When they got closer, one of the soldiers turned around. "Go away, boys of Greeve," he said, his voice oddly accented.

Lex made a series of sounds like birdcalls. "Now!" he said.

Nort clapped his hands over Lex's ears and Lex covered his eyes with his own hands just as the soldier watching them snorted. The soldier giggled. And chortled. And guffawed. The soldier next to him began to laugh, and the next man, and the next. Soon the entire rear squadron was laughing, slapping their knees and grunting. One of them laughed like an insane horse. Someone else squeaked. One by one the soldiers fell down and rolled around, still laughing.

"Quartz and feldspar, granite and graphite," Lex intoned solemnly. "Seven times eight is fifty-six."

Nort pushed Lex forward, stepping between the fallen soldiers. Ahead of them, the men were dropping in ranks, and the sound of their laughter began to drown out Lex's voice. "Don't smile, don't smile," Nort told Lex, even though Lex couldn't hear him.

They trudged forward. In a matter of moments, Nort and Lex were nearly to the castle. Noblemen and kings lay on the ground before the castle gates, laughing themselves breathless. Beyond them, puzzled faces looked out through the heavy iron grating.

Then one of the kings rolled right under Lex's feet, and both boys stumbled over him and fell. Lex's ears were freed. His eyes flipped open. At the sight and sound of the hysterical army, Lex himself laughed.

All of the other laughter stopped. The soldiers rose to their feet in a great, angry mass, brushing themselves off.

"Oops," said Nort as the two kings glared at him and the young wizard. One of the kings raised his sword.

Lex nearly doubled over laughing, all by himself. Nort nudged him.

The kings had lifted their eyes to look past the boys. Nort and Lex turned around to see why.

Behind them, the soldiers parted ranks, whispering. A single figure rode up to the castle gates, a delicate woman on a mule.

Though Queen Istilda was no longer sixteen, she was certainly a damsel in distress. Her fair hair curled about her shoulders, her lips trembled, and her blue eyes filled with tears. "Good sirs," she cried out as she stopped before the invading monarchs, "you have come to our aid!"

King Jal lowered his sword. "Well now. What seems to be the trouble?" he asked.

The queen looked from one king to the other. "You're not from Rogast, are you?"

"Tark of Tarylon," the second king said, saluting gallantly.

"Jal of Lors," said that doughty man.

The queen let out her breath. Another tear crept down her cheek. "I am Queen Istilda, and young Vantor of Rogast has dealt with my kingdom most grievously."

The kings stepped closer, lowering their formidable brows. "What has he done?"

"May I offer you some refreshment while I tell the tale?" the queen said, indicating the castle gates with one slender hand.

The kings exchanged guilty glances. "Certainly," said Tark.

"Splendid idea," Jal put in.

At a signal from the queen, the gates opened wide.

At a signal from the kings, the army surrounding the castle fell back a bit.

The queen caught sight of Nort. "Ah, my young retainer," she said. Her sharp eyes focused on Lex. "And his delightful companion. Won't you join us?"

King Jal frowned. "If I'm not mistaken, that boy's a wizard."

"Yes," Istilda said. "Perhaps he might be of use."

Lex and Nort followed the monarchs into the castle.

In the late afternoon sunlight, dust blew across the farmyard. A handful of chickens squawked anxiously, scattering into the grass by the fence. White curtains blew softly out of open windows. The scene lacked only hoofbeats. It got footbeats instead, as Vantor and his men tramped up to the fence, knocking the gate right down.

"You five keep the king and his fops over there by the barn," Vantor ordered. "If I don't come out with the princess, you know what to do."

"Leave Meg alone!" Dilly cried, struggling against one of her captors.

"Gag that one, too," Vantor added.

The guards pushed their prisoners toward the barn. "Move along!"

Vantor strode across the yard, then struck a proud pose before the house. "Princess, come out!" he commanded in deep, royal tones.

Meg stuck her head out the window. "You've got to be kidding!" she said. Meg pulled her head back in and slammed the shutters.

"Um, Vantor's here," she told the others.

"That arrogant lout?" Janna demanded.

Meg nodded. "I'm not going anywhere with him!"

Vantor was yelling something outside the door. They could hear footsteps as the prince's men surrounded the house.

"Close the shutters!" Janna cried. The four of them hurried to secure the windows. Just in time, as heavy fists struck the shutters from the outside. The large room was gloomy now, bereft of sunlight.

"I won't let him take you," Cam said, snatching a toasting fork.

"You really need a knife," Meg told Cam.

"What weapons have we got?" Janna asked, looking around.

"Magic." Gorba flexed her wrinkled hands.

Meg felt the warm weight against her leg. "The dragon."

"That scarf of yours," Janna said.

"Frogs," Cam remarked, rolling his eyes.

Someone was banging on the door, but the farmhouse was sturdily built, and the door held.

"Come open a window for me," Gorba said to Cam, and he quickly obliged. Gorba stuck her head out. "Boo!" the witch said. The man outside reached in, but Gorba touched him, hissing an incantation. The attacker turned an amazing shade of pink and sprouted tentacles. He fell to the ground gurgling. Cam slammed the window shut.

"Can you do that to all of them?" Meg asked hopefully.

Gorba shook her head. "Takes a lot of magic. But it might scare a few of them off." Indeed, that particular window had gone rather quiet.

Then something struck the door harder, again and again. The tip of an ax appeared through the wood.

"Uh-oh," said Meg.

"With my own ax!" an indignant Janna cried.

"We need an army," Cam said.

Meg shrugged. "The frogs could jump on their heads."

"That's it, girl!" Gorba smiled maniacally.

"What's it?" Meg asked.

"We *have* an army!"

22

ING TARK SLAMMED HIS TEACUP DOWN ON THE table, where it shattered into minute rose-patterned pieces. The king turned red. "I'm sorry," he said, flustered. His jaw jutted. "But this Vantor is a disgrace to the name of prince."

King Jal nodded. "He must be stopped."

"After all," Queen Istilda pointed out, "it wouldn't do to set a precedent like this."

The two kings considered the implications of her words. Then Jal spoke. "We'll take care of the young upstart."

Tark cleared his throat. "There is another matter, the one that brought us to your fair dwelling."

Jal gazed around at the castle with a faintly disappointed air. "Right. Our sons."

"We received word that our boys had been enchanted," Tark went on.

"That fellow at the gate said frogs," Jal added.

Istilda sighed. "I'm afraid our contestants' efforts to deal with the witch went badly." Both men opened their mouths to speak, but she lifted her hand, and they subsided. "We must rescue not only my husband and daughter but your sons."

"Where is the witch?" Tark asked.

"I don't know," the queen admitted.

"Now, look here—" Jal began.

"But I believe this young man can help us discover her hiding place," Istilda said.

Everyone turned to look at Lex. He smiled, giving them a little wave.

"Well?" Her Majesty asked.

"Oh, sure. I can do that," Lex said.

The ax came clear through the door as Gorba hurried over to the row of milk pails. "Boys," she said in the tones of a general, "we need your help."

"Against a foul . . ." said Meg.

". . . treacherous . . ." said Cam.

". . . unworthy prince!" Janna finished.

The frogs stuck their heads up. Gorba whirled her hands, calling, "Princilio Heroish Ribbet!"

Suddenly the room was full of princes. Meg was relieved to see that they were all dressed, though some of their doublets resembled the ones in the oldest family portraits. Tall princes, short princes, fat and skinny princes, each one looking a little stunned.

"To battle!" Gorba cried.

None of the princes had any weapons, unfortunately. Janna began to arm them with fire pokers and spatulas. And not a moment too soon, as the door and most of the windows gave way. The transformed frogs took vigilant battle stances.

An instant later, Vantor and his men burst into the house, expecting to find a girl and a few farm folk.

Instead they faced a ring of angry princes.

Vantor stopped short. Then he smirked. "They have no swords!" Vantor stabbed at the nearest prince with his own sword, only to find air as the frog prince leaped right over his head. Vantor spun around. The prince kicked him hard in the chest with long, strong legs. Vantor fell. When he got up, the prince gave him a wide smile and jumped away to find another foe.

Vantor moved to follow, but a second prince tapped him on the shoulder with a wire whisk, and he was forced to defend himself again.

All through the room, frog princes were leaping and kicking, spinning and slamming and slashing and bashing.

Vantor's men weren't doing very well.

Some of them managed to corner Gorba behind the stove, but she kept reaching out to poke them with a large wooden spoon. One fell in a heap and started snoring. Another began reciting the *Epic of Lanolan* and couldn't stop himself. A third shrank down to a twelve-year-old boy, sprouting a ripe faceful of pimples.

Cam and Janna knelt behind the kitchen table,

throwing chili pepper into the noses of anyone who came near. Janna's cats yowled encouragement from the rafters.

The scarf got into the spirit of things, too, biting dozens of ears and noses and driving a terrified Beaknose out into the night.

As for Meg, she wielded a mean dragon. *Hit his knees!* she thought, barely managing to support chubby Laddy as she aimed him. Laddy obligingly spouted a gout of flame. The man who was lunging toward the princess fell back, howling.

The fight whirled through the room, breaking Janna's favorite pitcher, scattering firewood, and knocking over all but one of the milk pails, so that pond water spilled everywhere and the combatants found themselves sliding about. On the slick floor Vantor's men lost their balance, but the frog princes grew even more agile, gliding and spinning like ice skaters.

Soon nearly all of Vantor's men were down, many of them with smug princes sitting on their backs as if they were so many lily pads.

But Vantor fought on. Meg watched him battle one prince after another, managing to wound three of the former frogs. Meg was surprised to see that their blood was red, not green. Meg tugged Laddy closer to Vantor. *Toes!* she thought. Fire licked across the room. Vantor began to hop madly from one foot to the other. Still he slashed at the farm's defenders.

Sword! Meg thought, inspired. The next blast lit Vantor's weapon an incandescent red. He dropped it, howling, as two princes leaped across the room, knocking him down. It took three more to subdue him. He kept thrashing about, screaming imprecations.

Janna brought some rope from a cupboard. She and Cam helped the frog princes tie Vantor and his men up. Meg's friends used extra rope on Vantor. He stopped yelling only because they threatened to gag him. The prince was reduced to muttering darkly.

Across the room, Gorba's victims were still snoring and reciting and bursting out in pimples. Meg asked the witch to end the spells so those men could be tied up, too.

Finally Meg put down her dragon and walked up to Vantor. She had to tilt her head to look him in the eye. "I won the contest. I found the dragon—the live dragon," she said pointedly, "before you did, and took him away. I have the witch. That's two out of three. What's more, I have myself. Making three out of four, actually." She paused. "What have you got?"

Vantor smiled crookedly. "The king," he sneered. "Checkmate."

"Where is he?" Meg demanded.

"My men have him. If you come with me, they'll let him live."

"Not for long," Gorba remarked.

"Quiet, hag!" Vantor said.

"Hag?" Gorba said ominously, but someone else was speaking.

"Did I miss all the fun?" Bain leaned in the shattered doorway with a roguish grin.

The kings of Lors and Tarylon rode alongside Lex and Nort and the queen, for whom they'd kindly provided horses. Behind them, two hundred soldiers marched rank on rank. The queen had left the head housekeeper in charge of the castle, asking Dorn and Dagle to assist her. The twin princes had agreed unwillingly, wanting to join in the rescue effort themselves.

"I don't understand," King Jal said again, tapping his horse's flanks with his heels. "The witch is with the princess, but she isn't holding her captive?"

"The witch is a friend of Meg's," Lex said.

"You are speaking of the same witch who turned my boy into a frog?" Tark asked harshly.

Nort moved his horse a bit farther from the angry king as he attempted to explain. "Dilly says the witch warned the princes away, but they all jumped on her, so Gorba had to use her frog spell."

"Who is this Dilly person, and why are you defending the witch?" Jal demanded.

"A moment," said Queen Istilda. "I believe the young people are trying to tell us that the witch isn't hostile, and will easily be persuaded to return her prisoners to their natural state."

"That's right," Nort said, feeling less alarmed.

"I like the sound of that," said King Tark. "Counterspells can be a bear."

"Unlikely," Lex said, "though I once saw a counter-spell that was a hummingbird." But no one was listening.

Meg's mouth dropped open at the sight of the bandit.

"You *dare* to show your face here?" Vantor snarled.

"This from a true prince"—Bain wagged his finger—"who's been truly naughty."

Vantor jerked against the ropes, but they held.

"Four out of four," Meg murmured to Vantor. He hissed like an enraged basilisk.

Bain turned his attention to Meg. "I found someone you know outside, but he was keeping bad company. I'm afraid Feg and I had to knock a few heads together." He looked around the room. "Much like yourselves, it appears."

Bain stepped inside. King Stromgard's form filled the doorway. "Daughter, you're safe!" the king cried.

"Yes, Father."

The king hurried to Meg and gave her a suffocating hug. "Had me scared, Meg," he muttered into her hair.

"I know," Meg squeaked. Her father released her with a sigh of relief. "You called me Meg," she said.

"Did I?" The king smiled.

Meg heard voices outside. Dilly and a handful of the king's courtiers pushed through the door. The prime minister hung back behind the rest.

Dilly ran to Meg and hugged her. "How could you let that fool prince capture you?" Dilly scolded.

"Fool prince?" said Vantor with royal disdain. Everyone turned to stare at him. "What are you going to do now?" he inquired.

"I'm within my rights to have you hanged," said King Stromgard.

"And start a war with my brother?" Vantor asked, still menacing.

"I've a better idea," Gorba said, muttering as she stepped forward to touch the prince. He fell to the floor, a large, vomit-colored frog. After a shocked moment, he made as if to hop into the one milk pail that hadn't been tipped over.

"No," Gorba said. The frog looked back at her. "You're on your own," the witch said.

Vantor hopped sullenly toward the door and out across the farmyard. "If you see that one around, kill him," Janna told her cats, who had descended from their perch on the rafters.

"Thank you," Stromgard said to Gorba with a royal bow. "I apologize for disturbing your household this past week."

"Well," Gorba said, flustered, "see that you don't do it again."

"Never, madam."

Gorba beamed.

The king faced his daughter now. "Margaret, you were right. I'm . . ." He took a deep breath. "I'm sorry I didn't listen to you."

Meg felt her face grow warm. "I'm just glad you're

safe," she said, realizing that it was true. "Where's Mother?"

"She escaped. I was hoping she would get word to Hanak." The king stooped suddenly. "Who's this?"

Laddy, exhausted by all the flame-throwing, managed to lift his firelit eyes to the king. The king scratched the dragon's head, and the creature rumbled contentedly. "That's a good boy," His Majesty crooned. "The dragon left a baby?"

Meg shrugged. "I found him. Crawling through his mother's hoard."

"More than one chest, I presume," King Stromgard said ruefully.

"Eleven, I think. Large ones."

The king stood up. "Which reminds me—"

But Bain was gone.

Not even Meg noticed three sparks drifting through the room like golden dust motes.

King Stromgard soon sent his nobles off to the castle to find the queen. The frog princes took their prisoners out to the barn, where they discovered Bain's five captives already neatly bound. The princes set a guard. They found the pink-tentacled man and brought him to Gorba, who was busy dressing the wounds of the injured princes. Then they put the house in order while Janna tried to make enough dinner for everyone.

"Those boys were easier to feed when they were

frogs," Janna told King Stromgard, who hovered over
the soup pot while Meg and Cam set the table. There
weren't enough bowls for them all. Janna had to bring
out mugs and small pans to serve up the soup.

At last the princes were perched about the house eating dinner, having insisted that the ladies and the king
take the chairs at the kitchen table. The princes appeared
to have forgotten their table manners, slurping dread-
fully, but no one complained. Everyone was too glad of
their help.

As for Laddy, he got his very own bowl of soup.

"The Battle of Hookhorn Farm," Meg murmured.

"What?" Janna said.

"We should name the fight, like in a history book."

"The Defense of the Princess," Janna suggested.

Meg shook her head. "Makes me sound like I didn't
do anything."

"The Frog Warriors of Greeve?" said Cam.

Some of the princes chuckled. Red-haired George
the Fourth of Shervelhame snapped at a passing fly and
was clearly dismayed to find his tongue so short.

"You make a lovely supper," the king told Janna, patting his stomach with satisfaction.

"Why, thank you," said Janna.

"But we'd better get back to the castle. Margaret's
mother must be frantic."

That's when they heard the hoofbeats and the marching feet.

23

OT AGAIN!" CAM MOANED. THE PRINCES sprang up, a little battered, but ready for action. Outside, a trumpet fanfare sounded across the now-dark farmyard.

King Stromgard managed to open the door, a hasty new construction. His wife flew into his arms. "Darling!" she cried.

Behind her stood two kings. "Istilda, who are these people?" Stromgard asked his queen.

"Oh! They've come for their sons. And to help you. Do you need help?"

Meg pulled her parents into the room. "Mother!"

Everyone waited for the royal family of Greeve to finish hugging. As Istilda began explaining to her husband about the not-quite-invading army, Janna graciously invited the visiting monarchs inside.

Lex and Nort tagged along after the new arrivals, prompting yet another reunion. Cam and Dilly were pleased to finally meet the young wizard. Cam thanked Lex for designing the spell that saved him, diplomatically avoiding reference to Lex's original magic. Nort remembered to tell the others about Dagle's poetry, and they all laughed at the thought of the twin princes proclaiming their love to an empty tower.

For their part, Jal and Tark appeared astonished at the quantity of princes lounging about the farmhouse, talking about the recent battle and the best-tasting kinds of flies. Jal went about from prince to prince, eventually focusing on one young face. "Edgley? Is that you, boy?"

The prince straightened up. "Why, Father!"

Meanwhile, Tark had found his own heir, Illipe, and was telling him just how to deal with witches in the future. Tark didn't seem to notice that Gorba was peering over his shoulder, listening avidly, and Illipe was wise enough not to mention it.

Meg looked around the room, well content. "We did it!" she said.

"Even with that Vantor around," Dilly boasted.

"And Bain," Cam added. "Why did he pretend to be a prince?"

"To get the dragon gold," Lex guessed. He sighed wistfully. "The spells I could have worked with all that treasure . . ."

"Don't you want to meet an actual dragon?" Meg asked.

"That's right!" Lex crowed. "Where is it?"

Meg led her friends over to the hearth, where Laddy and the cats and Meg's scarf were snoozing in a heap now that the excitement had died down. Lex knelt to pat the baby dragon. "Their hearts are said to make a man invincible."

"Don't even think about it!" Meg warned.

"What about a scale?" Lex wheedled.

Laddy opened one eye, sneezing a thread of flame.

"Look, he dropped one," Cam said. He picked the scale up from the hearthstones. It shimmered red and gold. Cam handed it to Lex.

"There you go," said Meg.

"I must say, being your co-conspirator is immensely satisfying." Lex slipped the scale into his pocket. "Now I really must talk to your friend the witch."

Gorba was helping Janna tidy the kitchen.

"Excuse me, madam witch," said Lex.

"You're that wizard boy," Gorba announced with some suspicion.

"It is an honor to meet such a brilliant practitioner of magic," Lex said, bowing.

Gorba blushed. "Well, some have called me that, yes, though not recently, at least not so as I can recall."

"I'm told the frogs were superb."

"It *is* my signature spell."

"I was wondering if I might come to see you, perhaps partake of your wisdom," Lex said.

"I suppose you might," the witch responded regally.

A frog hopped down into the rushes beside the pond on Hookhorn Farm. He was surprised to find a welcoming committee—a dozen wet curving shapes with gleaming red eyes. The frog hesitated.

"What's the matter, Vantor?" Horace asked. "Scared of a few salamanders?"

In the farmhouse, things had calmed down once more, and some of the princes started hinting at Gorba to change them back into frogs. Kings Jal and Tark caught wind of this and, reluctant to attack a witch who was obviously a guest of the household, instead began giving heart-wrenching speeches about grieving parents in kingdoms throughout the land. By the time they were finished, most of the princes had promised to go home.

Some of the older princes figured they'd been gone so long they were no longer missed; they decided they would set off together in search of adventure the next morning.

Everyone agreed it was too late to go back to the castle. After a bit of shuffling and fussing, Janna managed to find makeshift bedding for most of her royal guests. They settled down in the farmhouse and the barn, while Jal's and Tark's soldiers set up camp in the cow pastures, to the great surprise of the cows.

The sun rose the following day to the welcome smell of pancakes—Janna's solution to her quantity of unexpected company. After breakfast, most of the frog princes bade fond farewells to the witch, who grew positively misty-eyed watching them go.

"I'll be back to visit," the last one promised. He couldn't have been much older than Cam.

Gorba waved her black hankie as all of the princes except Edgley and Illipe set off. She patted her pocket, sniffing. "It's all right, Howie."

Then Gorba's bright eyes caught sight of Meg across the room with her friends. She frowned, watching Meg and Cam.

The witch went to pack her things.

A few minutes later, Meg found her. "Can I help?"

Gorba shook her head.

"I'm sorry about your frogs."

"Time the boys stopped hopping about and got on with their lives." The witch tucked a handful of vials into her knapsack. "That bandit was a nice-looking fellow, wasn't he?" she asked innocently.

Meg stiffened. "I hadn't noticed."

In the farmhouse kitchen, three monarchs gathered for an informal meeting. "No more of these contests, eh, Stromgard?" Tark said, slapping the king of Greeve on the back with a jovial air.

"No more of these unannounced visits with hundreds of soldiers, heh heh," Stromgard replied, slapping Tark's back in turn.

All three rulers exchanged shrewd looks. Queen Istilda noticed wryly that the kings of Tarylon and Lors weren't rushing to introduce their sons to her daughter. She kept her thoughts to herself, though, thanking the visitors yet again for their heroic assistance. At last Jal and Tark, sons in tow, marched away to their own realms, promising not to leave any armies lying around behind them.

Everything else was soon sorted out, and the royal family of Greeve made their way home to the castle, where the king relieved Dorn and Dagle of guard duty. The twin princes were rather woebegone, having learned about the dragon and other recent developments from one of the servants.

When the king thought to ask where his guards were, the queen explained that she and her royal companions had met some of Hanak's men on the road to the farm. Part of that squad was put in charge of the prisoners from the barn. As it turned out, Hanak and the rest of his men returned to the castle much later without a single glimpse of a bandit, let alone of Vantor or the princess.

Hanak was appalled to find out all that had happened without him. It took the king a great deal of talk to convince the loyal captain that his absence from the Battle of Hookhorn Farm was only a matter of unfortunate timing. "Besides," the king said, "Prince Bain was a great help."

Hanak gritted his teeth. "I understand, Sire."

King Stromgard also had a long meeting with his abashed prime minister, charging him never to use the words "economic development" again. In the weeks to come, Garald was often seen with a thesaurus, trying to come up with an acceptable alternative.

The king further commanded Garald to plan suitable rewards for those who had helped keep his daughter safe during the past week. By applying his imagination, not to mention asking Meg for her advice, the prime minister did a fine job of selecting rewards for the princess's companions. The king approved each and every one.

Nort was to be trained under Hanak's direct supervision, with an eye toward eventual knighthood. "A promising lad," Hanak growled, "but he's going to learn *whose* orders to follow *when!*"

"Yes, sir," Nort said fervently.

After Dilly had survived a little talk with her uncle about using his name to improperly influence guards, she was given the title of Meg's lady-in-waiting. Dilly was specifically assigned not to carry towels. She was given some satin gowns of her very own, which she hung carefully in her airy new chamber. "Do I have to gossip?" Dilly asked Meg, eyeing the queen's bevy of ladies.

To Chief Gardener Tob's amazement, Cam was allowed to pick his own section of the palace gardens to manage. Meg wasn't surprised when her friend chose the kitchen gardens. "Roses are nice," he confided, "but there's nothing like the orange curve of a fine pumpkin or the snap of a good green bean."

Gorba kindly agreed to make the king's tower and the houses in Crown visible again. Then she went back to her wood, which the king deeded to her officially. Before she left, though, Gorba magically repaired Janna's pitcher and promised to come to tea with her at least once a week to discuss Greevian literature. Janna had quickly recovered from the shock of having her farm attacked. The king sent a crew of laborers to repair Hookhorn Farm. In addition, he bought Janna more cows and pigs and named her Guardian of the Royal Dragon.

Meg didn't want to leave Laddy at the farm, but she had to admit he was safer there than at the castle, where not everyone seemed to understand how sweet he was. *I'll come see you all the time*, Meg told him.

The king tried to name Lex Royal Wizard. Lex said no thank you, but he would always be available for contract work. "I'm an independent man," Lex told Meg later. "When are you coming over for hot chocolate?"

Since the king wanted to reward Bain for saving his life and Hanak wanted to throw Bain in the dungeons, the prime minister wasn't sure what to do. The decision was taken out of his hands, however, because the bandits were seen no more in the kingdom of Greeve. Except once—and Meg was the only person who knew about that.

First the princess had a discussion with her parents about her own future. Meg wore her scarf for courage.

The king leaned forward over his desk. "What's that around your neck?"

"A magic scarf."

"It appears to be watching me," King Stromgard said.

"Yes. It saved my life."

The king and queen exchanged glances.

"Gorba gave it to me," Meg added.

"I see." The king sat back, but he kept his eyes on the scarf.

"Now then," Queen Istilda said. "As you well know, you've caused us a great deal of worry these past few days. You've been disobedient and underhanded."

"I'm sorry to have frightened you," Meg said honestly.

"Therefore, we are not going to reward you publicly for your actions," the queen said.

Meg drooped. Maybe everything was going to be like before.

"Nevertheless," her father continued, "your actions have shown us that you have the makings of a monarch."

Meg looked up, surprised.

"Your mother feels that you have become sufficiently

adept at embroidery to move on to other studies, sub-
jects such as administration and diplomacy," the king
said.

"What?" Meg asked, worried.

"Don't forget," her mother put in.

"Ah yes. Also magic, horsemanship, and swordplay."

Meg felt a smile spreading across her face, bright and
warm as a baby dragon.

Across the valley, a cow ambled up to the gate of a farm.
An old woman came out to greet her. "Why, you silly
thing. What happened to your two fine friends?"

"I hate to question the decisions of a lady queen," Dorn
told his brother as they climbed back up the mountain,
"but she should have taken us along."

"To the battle?"

Dorn nodded. "Instead of leaving us in the castle
with that terrifying woman."

"Our mother's housekeeper is much more gentle,"
Dagle agreed.

They reached the dragon trap and stood looking at it
mournfully.

"If I hadn't seen the bones myself, I would still have
high hopes for our handiwork," said Dorn.

"One of the guardsmen says there's a baby, but he's
too young to fly."

Dorn considered this. "We could wait."

"Or," Dagle told him, "we could find another king-dom with dragon troubles."

Dorn's eyes lit up. "And make another trap!"

"Exactly!"

Dorn surveyed their camp with renewed determina-tion. "All right," he said briskly. "We'll leave the wood and take the tools."

In a small room over a tavern somewhere on one of the winding streets of Crown, a minstrel messed about, try-ing out new words to a very old melody.

"O, the princess was trapped in the tower high,
But she spread her wings 'gainst the jewel–blue sky . . .

"No, that's not good. Here now . . .

"But with wings of magic she did fly . . .

"Awkward. What about . . .

"The princes rode through the castle gate,
While the maiden in the tower did wait . . .

"Better. For now.

"But in the night . . .

"Nope.

"But not for long . . .

"Pah!"

The minstrel laid his lute on the narrow bed and went downstairs, letting the words roll around and around in his head, knowing that soon enough they would turn themselves into a song.

EPILOGUE

WEEK AFTER THE ROYAL FAMILY RETURNED from their adventures, the castle was still buzzing over all of the goings-on in Greeve. Tired of the fuss one night, Meg took a lantern and went down to the frog pond. She thought about bringing Cam along, but decided she wanted to be alone, dreaming new dreams.

The frogs' eyes gleamed in the rays of her lantern. Meg wondered if any of them had ever been princes.

"I heard a strange story," someone said behind her. "A new lute ballad, actually."

Meg turned around. Bain was leaning against a tree, watching her.

"Why do you lean like that?" she asked him.

Bain laughed and came to stand beside her, carrying a cloth-wrapped object. "For the effect, I suppose."

"It's not working," she told him. "What story did you hear?"

"About a bold princess who escaped from her tower without anyone knowing."

"Cam says tales aren't always true," Meg said primly.

"How is that princess?" Bain asked. "Is she living happily ever after?"

Meg grinned. "She's learning swordplay."

"Apt," Bain told her.

"What about you?"

"We're going away. Alya wants a new life for our people."

"Your sister, the Bandit Queen. So why aren't you the Bandit King?"

"I'm the prince," Bain said, strutting a bit.

"Hmmph. Lex says you were just after the gold."

"Maybe. Or maybe Feg thought my imitation of a noble fop was so amusing that he jeeringly suggested I could pass as a prince in the royal contest. Naturally, he would come to regret his words."

Meg laughed. "Naturally."

Bain changed the subject. "I brought you a present. A person who wins a contest should get a prize."

"She should," Meg said, pleased. "It wouldn't be those chests of treasure, would it?"

"Sorry. That's Alya's concern. But I did steal a little something for you."

"Thief," Meg said mildly.

"This from the girl who stole herself, not to mention a dragon and a witch. Here." Bain placed the long packet in her hands.

"Thank you."

"You're welcome. Goodbye, Princess."

"It's Meg, to my friends."

Bain smiled. "Goodbye, Meg." He faded into the darkness, a shadow lost in the shadows. Meg waited at least a minute before she opened the package. In the lantern light she could see that her gift was a strong, slender sword, its silver hilt scored with sigils and set with moonstones. Meg lifted it to the night. "Once upon a time," she said, "there was a princess who knew she was meant for more than twirling her tresses and swooning."